The Krybosian Stairpath

Magnetic Reversal

S. R. R. Colvin

Interior art by Carolyn Bradley

iUniverse, Inc.
New York   Bloomington

The Krybosian Stairpath
Magnetic Reversal
2nd edition

iUniverse books may be ordered through booksellers or by contacting:

iUniverse
1663 Liberty Drive
Bloomington, IN 47403
www.iuniverse.com
1-800-Authors (1-800-288-4677)

Because of the dynamic nature of the Internet, any Web addresses or
links contained in this book may have changed since publication and
may no longer be valid. The views expressed in this work are solely those
of the author and do not necessarily reflect the views of the publisher,
and the publisher hereby disclaims any responsibility for them.

ISBN: 978-1-4401-5927-5 (pbk)
ISBN: 978-1-4401-5928-2 (ebk)

Library of Congress Control Number: 2009932970

Printed in the United States of America

iUniverse rev. date: 2/5/2010

Acknowledgments

Many people deserve mention here. First are my three children, Dana, Carly Dawn, and Caitie. They were the original inspiration for me writing a children's book, and they continue to inspire me to improve myself and my world. They loved to read and I loved to read to them. And during the final stages of this book, all three were pregnant and ready to provide me with three more readers.

My grandchildren also served as an inspiration in the writing of this book. They are Taylor, Austin, Madison, and the newest three, Jacqi, Abby, and Aurora. Madison is my little angel in heaven, sitting in the comfort of God's lap, where she was the first to read Grandma's finished book.

I owe a huge debt to Jim, my African hunter, for his constant encouragement through a period when I was too worn out from work and family matters to stay up and write. He encouraged me through many revisions that became necessary when another writer published several works over the course of nine years that contained material from my original story. The repeated plot and scene changes nearly derailed this entire project. If not for Jim, this book may never have made it into print.

When few others would read my manuscript, Jim jumped right in and read it. Sadly, the ending wasn't written at that time, and he came looking for the rest of the book.

You should have seen the look on his face when he discovered he had just digested 18 chapters with no end in sight. I love him so.

Many thanks to the following people: Angie Gautier, Tracy Goad, Brenda Lamb, Toni Trueheart, Nancy Litz, Gerald McPeak, Peggy Murphy, Jolene Mabrey, Candice Johnson, Tommy Lawson, Brian Spraker, and Kevin Jones. Kevin was always happy to read a chapter and was always full of . . . ideas . . . on possible revisions. These people put up with my exhausted whining at work during the period of major revisions.

Joan and Henry Bolduc offered words of encouragement on the publishing process, and sometimes, I really needed it. And as always, my brothers Richard and Robert were instrumental in propelling me forward.

Many thanks go to Linda Hutchins Vidar for her editing efforts on my manuscript. Her advice helped me to expand it where it was thin, and strengthen it where it was weak. And a special thanks to Carolyn Bradley, whose artistic ability enabled the world to see the kids that had lived in anonymity, in my head for so many years.

Most of all, I owe a tremendous debt to my mother and father, Marian and Bill. They advocated reading and education from the earliest days of my life. Thanks Mom and Dad!

S.R.R. Colvin

Dedication

To Jim, with all my love. Thanks for the endless encouragement when I needed it most.

1
A Tale to Tell

"The morning wind ripped through my jacket with the ease of a knife slicing through water. I was near exhaustion, but knew I had to keep going. The climate grew increasingly desperate with each passing hour and, come nightfall, the entire world of Krybos would be uninhabitable. I knew that I'd become the only hope of reversing what had been set into motion earlier that day." Rocky Terrence paused briefly as if to contemplate a different outcome, then leaned forward in his chair and continued his story.

"I stretched my collar up as high as it would go and pressed on toward the tunnel entrance to Mount Zaltana. Mourgla, the evil mastermind of this impending destruction, trailed only minutes behind me, and he planned to stop me. That's when it happened."

"What, Grandpa? What happened?" Mica Terrence

begged for more of the story. His enthusiasm for Grandpa Rocky's fabulous tales never waned. Mica loved an adventurous tale of mystery and terror. Oh, what he wouldn't give for an adventure of his own!

"Great gophers," Grandpa said. "I'm afraid we'll have to finish this one later, Mica. Your sister needs us over at the library."

Not far away, eleven-year-old Madison Terrence found herself in a bad situation, not realizing it could easily have been much worse. Her anger and emotional desperation generated a powerful, invisible signal that crossed the small town of Cavern City, Virginia to reach Grandpa Rocky and Mica.

"Gees," Mica said, shaking his head in disappointment. He knew they had to get going because he had also received his older sister's call for help. This remote sensing ability to know when others were in danger came from Grandpa. He'd learned it during his youthful travels and had recently begun to instruct Mica and Madison on how to master it.

However, this ability came with a warning that it must always remain a family secret. And that's just what Madison didn't want, or need. *More secrets!*

Soon, Madison would find herself on a collision course with her family's mysterious past, and her own ultimate destiny. It had all started earlier in the day, with that substitute teacher....

2
Dead Time

They must be dead! Madison thought. She'd never seen the hands on a clock move so slow that they seemed stationary. *Come on—move!* She tried to wish it back into service.

With the clock on the classroom wall stalled at four minutes to 3:00 PM, Madison squirmed in her desk as if the seat scorched her bottom. She loved school, and usually dreaded summer break, but this year was different. Madison had a mission. She planned to spend the entire summer solving what she called the "Terrence Family Mystery" that had surrounded them for years.

Odd and sometimes unexplained occurrences shadowed her whole family. Because of it, Madison endured an endless onslaught of taunting and ridicule by her schoolmates, and by the town locals. Some people even seemed to be afraid of the Terrences.

Part of this mystery involved Madison herself. She had always been targeted by the kids in town because of her uncanny intelligence. But this year seemed, to her, to be the worst ever.

Madison ached to be normal. She couldn't help it if she remembered everything she ever saw or read. She didn't know why; she just could. Her teachers thought it was odd, but wonderful. Classmates thought it was really weird, and persecuted her because of it.

When Madison tried to disguise her gift, it always backfired. If she pretended that she didn't know the answer to a question, someone would say something so incredibly stupid that it caused her to blurt out the correct answer, just to put a stop to the nonsense.

The one person who did not think it odd at all was Grandpa. But he had a reputation for being a little eccentric, so of course he'd think it was normal. It was Grandpa Rocky who, in his youth, built the Terrence family fortune on the old rock quarry he ran at the end of the street still named for it. But, the quarry had flooded some fifty years ago leaving Grandpa no choice but to lay off the workers and barricade its entrance. Strangely, fifty years was exactly how long those mysterious stories and rumors had circulated about the Terrence family. Madison thought that was long enough.

This summer she intended to unravel the mystery, starting with a search of the school library archives. She knew there must be a local history book, newspaper article, or some sort of record that would reveal a clue.

"Stop it!" Madison demanded. She twirled in her seat to see what the warped kid behind her was doing now. As she spun around, her head snapped to a sudden stop and she yelped, "Ouch!"

"What?" Jacin Means asked innocently. He leaned back holding his hands up and trying to look genuinely surprised by her outburst.

"I didn't do nuttin'," Jacin said to the teacher, but the crooked smirk on his face revealed his true pleasure in having tied Madison's hair to the slats in the back of her chair.

The classroom erupted in laughter as Madison tried frantically to free herself.

Jacin chose the seat behind Madison on purpose because he enjoyed making her life as miserable as he possibly could. When she tried to switch seats at the beginning of the school year, the teacher wouldn't allow it.

If only that bell would ring. Madison refocused her attention on the clock that appeared to click off years instead of minutes. She wanted to get as far away from Jacin as she could, as quickly as she could. *Three more minutes,* Madison thought.

With the countdown commencing, she took a deep breath and pressed her shoulders against the hard wooden back of her desk chair. She slid down in the seat, trying to be invisible until she was free for the summer.

A tall woman with poofy hair, styled like the girls' in old Elvis Presley movies, stood at the front of the class. Madison thought this substitute teacher wore too much makeup, and a purple dress too long out of style, for a woman in her twenties. To Madison at least, she seemed out of place—or out of time. Unusual as it was to have a substitute on the last day of school, Madison was glad.

Maybe, being a stranger, this woman wouldn't be singling her out to answer questions in front of everyone.

Moving to the blackboard, the teacher pinched the chalk in her fingers and drew a symbol on the smeary, streaky mess remaining after a week of writing and erasing chalk. After only a few strokes, Madison recognized the drawing as an ancient religious symbol of mysterious origin.

Great, Madison thought. She cringed in disbelief. *No way anyone in this room will guess this one.*

With the drawing complete, the substitute rotated on her heels and stopped to face the class. "Who knows what this is?" She extended her arm toward the symbol and turned her palm up as she lightly gripped the chalk, using it as a pointer.

It became obvious to Madison from the wave of bowed heads moving across the room and the sea of blank faces surrounding her that no one knew what it was. No one, that is, except her.

I'm not going to answer. I'm not going to answer, Madison repeated to herself.

Teachers always depended on her for facts and information. She liked 'knowing things,' but hated that it made her look like the teacher's pet. Not just *a* teacher's pet, but *every* teacher's pet. She tried ducking her head whenever a teacher asked a question, hoping to go unnoticed, but they knew where she sat. So when no one else could produce the answer, Madison would hear her name called. Instantly every head in the room turned to glare at her for being a know-it-all. Madison hated the attention.

But this time, she thought she enjoyed anonymity. The substitute didn't know her, and she would escape the final humiliation of the 2009 school year.

"No one knows?" The substitute scanned every face around the room as she maneuvered through the rows of desks. Suddenly she halted, and said, "I'll bet you know."

"Yea, book-babe, what's the answer?" A voice chided Madison from across the room and stirred another round of laughter at her expense.

Madison glanced up in disbelief. The odd-looking teacher leaned in and stared her square in the eye. It was the kind of stare a person could feel like a laser burning a path through its victim. Mesmerized, Madison struggled to regain control of herself. That's when she saw the teacher's hand inching toward the chalcedony crystal dangling from her necklace.

"Well...." Madison's voice trailed off as she wrapped her fingers protectively around her gem, and leaned away from the intruder.

What is going on here? Madison wondered. She couldn't be sure whether the woman meant to steal her gemstone or simply admire it. After all, it was a rare treasure. What Madison found really amazing was that a complete stranger had managed to single her out.

Rrrrrrrring! The final bell of the school year sang out.

Instantly, the classroom became a whir of noise and movement as students ran clamoring for the door, with Madison in the lead.

3
Madison's Treasure

"I'm outta here!" Mica proclaimed as he darted past his sister, hoping not to get stopped for running in the hall. He was on his way to meet Grandpa Rocky, who waited on the sidewalk in front of the school. Mica and Grandpa were going downtown to play video games at the arcade.

"Whatever." Madison barely acknowledged him as he flashed past her. She had no interest in games and had never even been to the arcade. So, while they ventured into town, she headed straight for the school library and its archives. She would meet up with them later at the public library, just down the street from the school. But first, she would spend some time mining for information before the library closed for the summer.

"Ah-choo!" Madison sneezed and sniffled as she sifted through every paper and magazine in the archives, including some blanketed with a thick layer of dust. It seemed like no one else had touched this collection since the school library was built. And yet, nearly a year's worth of the local newspaper was missing.

"Miss Slonaker?" Madison leaned out of the archive room looking for the librarian.

"Child, it's the start of summer break. Why are you still here?" Sylvia Slonaker was more of a bookworm than Madison, but even she knew there were other matters just as important.

"I'm doing some research," Madison said. "I noticed that most of the *Cavern City Gazette* from 1959 is missing."

"That's strange—very strange," Miss Slonaker replied. She shifted her eyes upward from the book she'd been trying to repair and peered over the rim of her bifocals.

"Great, *another* mystery," Madison said as she slid her book bag off of the table and slung it over her shoulder. She waved her hand above her head as she left the library.

"Have fun this summer, but don't forget to keep reading!" Miss Slonaker stood and leaned toward the door in an attempt to force her voice down the hall.

By the time Madison emerged from the school, the parking lot was almost empty except for several teachers' cars. Students and parents alike had wasted no time leaving the grounds that day. Madison turned and made her way toward the public library, dodging sidewalk cracks and pondering the process that makes concrete expand and contract. Madison liked to analyze everything. She wanted things to make sense to her. If they didn't, she read and researched until they did make sense.

Suddenly, a weird feeling crept up inside Madison. It was a feeling that someone might be watching, or worse, following her! Without missing a step, she turned slightly to peer back over her shoulder. For a moment, Madison thought she saw a shadowy figure dart behind a building, just beside the school. She continued on her way, but was beginning to be very rattled by the creepy feeling that haunted her. Every few yards Madison turned her head to be sure that no one was following her. She thought she caught a glimpse of a tall figure, wearing a dark purple robe and hood, as it vanished into the surroundings. She stopped and scanned behind her, but saw no one.

Okay, that's weird. Madison thought. *Nobody dresses like that around here, especially not in a warm month like June.* She shrugged it off as a trick of the light, playing in the shadows cast by the tree leaves. She thought this was a reasonable explanation. However, Madison's scientific approach to earthly matters left her ill-prepared, and in constant danger from other-worldly forces. The events of this day had been leading Madison toward a sinister encounter.

A dangerous shadowy menace was drawing closer to her. It lurked behind one of the large oaks that grew in a neat, grassy row, separating the sidewalk from the road. The figure had crept up just behind Madison and threw back its hood to reveal a nightmarish face. As it reached for her throat, she stopped in her tracks.

"Freak!" blurted a tall, thin boy as he stepped out from behind a shrub and into her path.

"Uneducated jerk!" Madison shot back.

"I wasn't talking to you. I was talking to your

freakazoid friend, behind you," Jacin said. "Good grief! I mean, that was too weird, even for *your* family!"

"What are you blabbering about?" Madison whirled around and surveyed the length of the sidewalk as far as she could see. There was nobody there.

She'd carried this feeling of being stalked all the way down the street, only to find Jacin blocking her way to the library. Jacin could always be counted on to cause trouble, and he always seemed to be causing it for her. Naturally, she assumed he was the explanation for her creepy feeling, so—with that mystery solved—she thought no more about it.

"What worse fate could possibly befall me today?" Madison's voice oozed with sarcasm.

Then she heard it. Clink! The clasp on her necklace broke and her beloved gemstone fell to the sidewalk, landing at Jacin's feet. Before she could react, he snatched it up in his bony hand.

"You give that back!" Madison demanded. She gritted her teeth. Her long blonde ponytail and neatly pressed clothes offered no clue to the fury that lay within. No one was as skilled as Jacin when it came to bringing it out of her. Not one to play games, she boiled with rage to be targeted by the meanest kid in her school. She thought he just might be the meanest kid on the planet! It seemed to her that everyone at school made fun of her uncanny intelligence and the Terrence family's peculiarities, but it was Jacin who enjoyed doing it the most.

"You give it back or I'll *take* it back."

Madison repeated her demand in a voice that climbed to a shrill pitch. It did that whenever she became angry or frustrated. And at that moment she felt angry, frustrated, and dead serious. Of course, she was always quite serious. A no-nonsense, straight-A student, her idea of an entertaining afternoon was reading college geology textbooks.

"What's the big deal? It's just some stupid rock." Jacin smiled with pride.

He smirked as he held the necklace with its bright green and red speckled stone high over his head, far out of its owner's reach. Jacin was very tall even for a 5th grader, and he used that to his advantage whenever he could. "Maybe this dumb ol' rock has some of those secret powers I've heard folks talking about," Jacin teased. He lowered the necklace slightly to take a closer look at the strange red flecks embedded deep inside. "It sort of looks like your friend's face."

"What friend would *that* be, you mush-brained moron?" Madison asked. She reasoned that since he was picking, it was more than fair for her to pick back. She had no idea who, or what, Jacin had seen sneaking up behind her just a few minutes earlier.

She realized that no amount of demanding or reasoning with this fool would help her to rescue the necklace, so Madison sprang into the air, grasping desperately to reach it. Jacin strained in a tall stretch and held her treasure even higher. With each jump, Madison made a desperate attempt to dislodge her necklace from the filthy hands of the most obnoxious kid she'd ever met. With each landing, her shiny golden ponytail grew looser and looser until its elastic wrap hit the sidewalk and her hair revealed its true length.

Madison always wore her hair up in a single ponytail,

to avoid sitting on it. She also liked being able to divide her ponytail and stuff half in each of the back pockets of her shorts. This made perfect sense to her, since the pockets must be there for something. Everything had to make sense, for Madison.

"What's the big *hairy* deal?" Jacin laughed at Madison coming undone. "It's just some stupid old rock, right?" He held the necklace higher, working it up between his long pale fingers until it lay pinched between their bony tips.

To Madison, the unusually large piece of chalcedony on her treasured necklace was *not* just some old stupid rock. It was a rare gemstone, given to her by Grandpa. Last summer she had spotted the beautiful gem encased in a tall glass cabinet in the attic. It was an odd-shaped stone with edges like a puzzle piece, but it seemed to Madison to be very special. Although quite reluctant at first, Grandpa agreed to make the gem into a necklace for her, and it had hung around her neck ever since. Madison wore it with pride, and felt honored to be entrusted with a piece from Grandpa's carefully tended collection.

"I wouldn't hold that bloodstone too high, son, or you'll be finding out just what it can do." Grandpa hooted and cackled as he rolled up in his wheelchair.

Standing on the metal posts sticking out from behind the chair, Mica rode in like a competitor in a Roman chariot race. Although not too impressed that Grandpa and Mica were out on the streets playing childish games again, Madison breathed a sigh of relief that help had arrived. Grandpa's gift of remote sensing amazed Madison, since she could not explain it with facts or numerical data. It just worked, and she was glad.

Grandpa knew the gem in Jacin's hand would cause no harm—at least not by itself—but Jacin didn't. Members of the Means family were all mean-spirited and superstitious, and afraid of anything or anyone they didn't understand. Grandpa figured all he had to do was suggest that the gem might be dangerous, and Jacin would toss it as if it were a live snake squirming in his hand.

"Oh, this is going to be great!" Mica said. He was always willing to be in on a good joke.

Jacin had heard chilling stories told by his own father about Rocky Terrence, and those strange happenings at the quarry just before it closed down. Everyone in town knew about the disturbing stories. Grandpa himself had told some of those tales about his working days in the quarry, and the odd 'rock' collection stored up in his attic. Some townsfolk dismissed it all as just eccentric yarns told by a crazy old man. But others, like the Means family, always believed Grandpa had a mysterious connection with something other-worldly and frightening.

With growing concern that the bright green crystal might actually hold some sort of evil power, Jacin tossed it toward Madison.

"Take your stupid rock," Jacin mumbled. Then, he turned and walked away holding his head high and congratulating himself for another successful assault on a member of the weird Terrence family.

Madison drew both hands up toward her face and clasped them together just as the necklace came at her. Slowly, she opened her hands out in front of her to find the beloved gem safely inside. Content with its recovery, she looked up from her treasure and watched Jacin, the purveyor of evil, as he slinked down the sidewalk.

"I never thought I could actually hate another person, but I'm pretty sure I hate Jacin Means." Madison said. "At least I don't have to look at that fool for the whole glorious summer to come."

"Look Grandpa!" Mica shouted, pointing to a small bird flying high above the library. A single blue jay jerked its way through the sky in unusually awkward flight. "Is that bird jacked up, or what?"

The seemingly confused bird flew overhead in lazy, dizzy circles—up and down, around and around. It followed the high mountain skyline for a distance, and then it flipped in the air and continued flying in circles. As the bird disappeared in the distant sky, Grandpa's expression grew worried, having seen this phenomenon before.

"What do you think is wrong with it, Grandpa?" Mica scrunched his glasses up by wriggling his nose first to the left, and then quickly to the right.

"I'll tell you." Madison said. She enjoyed every opportunity to demonstrate her knowledge to Mica. She tilted her head back as if preparing to deliver a college lecture. "That bird is a Blue Jay, Latin name '*Cyanocitta cristata*,' and it exhibits the classic symptoms of West Nile Virus. It was probably bitten by a mosquito that hatched in the standing water down at the quarry. Mosquitoes carry the virus, and they generally lay their eggs in standing water."

Mica looked to Grandpa for reassurance about this mystery of the dizzy bird, while Madison waited for congratulations on her expert diagnosis. But Grandpa sat in silence, his head tilted to one side. He'd carried an ill feeling all afternoon. He felt an odd presence of someone, or something, that didn't belong in Cavern City. He rolled his lips inward over his teeth and then slowly let them return to normal. Then, without shifting his worried gaze from the skyline, Grandpa said, "That certainly is one possibility."

Grandpa knew exactly what that dizzy bird meant, and it had nothing to do with a virus. He'd seen it before, on that life-changing day when the quarry closed fifty years ago. But, he didn't want to arouse a lot of questions concerning matters the kids didn't need to know about, just yet. Grandpa reached out for the broken necklace and waved his hand in the direction of home. Mica and Madison took turns pushing Grandpa down Halite Street and onto Rock Quarry Road, where the Terrence home stood all alone at the very end.

4
Terrence Hall

"Listen to that—*it's creepy!*" Mica called out.

"I'm telling you, it's the virus," Madison insisted.

The songbirds had given up on their early morning symphony. Their weak chirps sounded like a warbling bird lover's clock as it drained the last ounce of energy from its battery. Sunlight streamed through the windows, delivering warmth to Mica's and Madison's bedrooms, at opposite ends of the third floor hallway. Dust bunnies played in the light, hovering just above the floor. If Mrs. Terrence could have seen them, someone would have been vacuuming.

The Terrence kids were usually up by now, even in the summer. But since this was the first day of summer break, they had both decided to stay in bed, just because they could. Mica and Madison lay across their beds and gazed out their front windows, looking for any signs of infected birds.

"Mom and Dad sure would be mad if they knew we were still in the bed." Mica sounded pleased with himself for sleeping in.

Jim and Linda Terrence never allowed the kids to sleep this late. However, they were away on a six-week trip to Arizona studying a strange eruption of earthquakes in an area that never had earthquakes before. As geology professors at the local university, Mr. and Mrs. Terrence spent their summer months doing research and usually, Madison and Mica went along. But this summer was different. Mr. Terrence said the kids couldn't go because of the extreme danger of what he called 'unpredictable crustal instability.' Madison and Mica didn't mind staying behind because they knew a summer with Grandpa Rocky would be a summer filled with interesting things to see, and endless fun.

"You know, Mica, Onyx will be here soon."

Madison was especially excited because her best friend, Onyx Ruiz, was arriving this morning from Peru to spend the summer. Madison met Onyx at the university, where the Terrences had hosted a geology conference almost two summers ago. Onyx's parents were also geologists, so she had accompanied them to Cavern City.

Thanks to Mica's acute sense of smell, Madison first met Onyx as she was eating lunch in the campus cafeteria. The smell of barbecued chicken had found its way down the long corridors from the cafeteria kitchen and right into Mica's nose. Madison was trying to soak up a speech being given by a world famous geologist, but had finally agreed to escort her brother to get some chicken, just so he would shut up about it.

As soon as Madison entered the dining area, she noticed the beautiful dark complexioned girl sitting alone. Onyx steadily nibbled on a big, sloppy American hamburger, but was paying more attention to the laptop computer open on the table in front of her. She had long hair like Madison, and appeared to be the same age. Onyx never looked up from her screen to notice Madison, who was trying to convince Mica to save some food for others. He was unusually small for an eight-year-old, but he possessed the appetite of a sumo wrestler.

Juggling Mica's overfilled tray of food, Madison guided him past Onyx's seat so that she could see the screen and what it was Onyx found to be so captivating. Assuming it was a mind-numbing video game similar to the ones Mica played, Madison nearly tripped and tossed the tray when she saw the complex physics computations filling the screen.

Madison, who usually had no interest in approaching people she didn't know, was suddenly intrigued. She left Mica to his feast and then bravely introduced herself. From that moment, she and Onyx became best friends, and ever since, they had spent their summers together. Last year Madison and Mica spent the summer with the Ruiz family in South America. This summer, Onyx would be Madison's guest while both sets of parents traveled to study the strange earthquakes occurring in the desert southwest.

Even Mica liked Onyx, which was unusual since he didn't care for hanging out with girls. Mica thought this girl was different because she was so daring, and she didn't seem to scare easy. She was smart like his sister, he thought, but not nearly so boring. He had actually looked forward to her visit.

Mica raised up a little from his bed as a faint, familiar squeaking sound became audible, and then increasingly louder. He shifted his gaze to the end of the street where he saw Arc Archaleous make his daily turn on to Rock Quarry Road.

"Hey, Maddy," Mica called down the hall. "That bike has been squeaking since last summer. Why doesn't he grease it?"

"Actually it's not a bike *or* bicycle, since a bicycle has two wheels—hence the Latin prefix *bi*—meaning *two*," Madison instructed. She sat up on her knees and turned toward her bedroom door to make sure that her brother could hear this Latin lesson at the other end of the hall. "It is actually a tricycle, Latin prefix 'tri,' meaning three. Mr. Archaleous' peddle-powered mail vehicle has three wheels. It's an adult-size tricycle."

"Big hairy deal!" Mica scowled, forcing his voice back down the hall. He hoped to remind her of yesterday's brush with Jacin in front of the library. "I don't care if it's a four-cycle! It still needs grease," he added. He offered this deliberate misuse of word prefixes, because he hated his sister's academic approach to everything.

Quad, Madison said to herself. Refusing to play Mica's childish games, Madison resisted the urge to correct his faulty language skills. She turned back toward the window and stretched out on her belly. Resting her chin in the palms of her hands, she watched Arc work his way down the street.

"Figures. The people with the biggest houses always seem to get the biggest mail. They even got a package," Mica grumbled. Arc stopped at a big brick house, where he emptied out one of the three mail baskets mounted on his mail trike.

"Must be somebody's birthday," Madison observed, as Arc stopped at a small white wooden house to drop off some brightly colored cards.

One mailbox at a time, Arc made his way past big homes, small homes, brick homes, wooden homes, big yards, flowery yards, and yards that looked like they hadn't been mowed since last summer.

Finally, Arc reached 241 Rock Quarry Road. It was an odd address, standing among the more normal look-ing houses in the neighborhood. 'Two forty-one' was no big brick house. It was no small wooden house. Its yard had no colorful flowers, and no grass overdue for mow-ing. Actually, there wasn't any grass at all in its yard, but only rocks—nothing but rocks.

The front yard of this home was a Zen Garden, made up entirely of rock. A sea of fine, clean gravel, raked to perfection with straight and wavy lines, filled the entire expanse of the front yard space, from the street up to the edge of the house. Large and uniquely shaped boul-ders were purposefully arranged in two groups in the level field of rock. They had their own wavy lines raked around them.

Through the middle of this rock garden, a winding walkway of carefully placed flagstone led visitors from the mailbox that stood by the street, to the massive front door of solid slate. The only plant life in sight was a patch of four-leaf clovers nestling at the base of the mailbox post.

If it weren't for the two upstairs windows and the two downstairs windows, the entire front of the house would have been nothing but rock, and probably its roof and sides as well. But only the front of the house could be seen, because the home at 241 Rock Quarry Road was built into the side of a mountain. Looking like nothing more than a flat prop from a movie set—a fake building front leaned up against a rocky cliff—the main part of 241's house was hidden underground.

"Looks like books for someone," Arc spoke to himself. He placed a small brown package from Amazon.com in the mailbox marked Terrence Hall, 241 Rock Quarry Road. Leaning back to sip from a frosty plastic bottle, he stretched out his arm and closed the mailbox door.

Waving to Arc from the upstairs windows, Mica and Madison caught his attention as he studied their strange house. Arc nodded hello and waved back to them. He capped his water bottle, and returned it to the cup holder on his handlebars. Then he turned and started back up Rock Quarry Road to finish his mail run.

As the familiar squeak of Arc's mail trike started to fade, another sound took its place. A muffled rattling, bumping, and creaking began in the room above their heads. Mica and Madison knew this all too familiar sound, and they leapt from their beds and raced down the hall.

"I'll take the stairs," Mica squealed with delight. He

bounded up the long spiral staircase skipping every other step.

"I'm taking the elevator, and I'll be waiting for you when you get there," Madison replied. Casually, she stepped inside and pressed a button marked with the letter *A*.

Next stop—Grandpa's Attic!

GRANDPA'S ATTIC

5
The Secrets in the Attic

This has to be some of the creepiest, and loveliest, stuff I've ever seen, Madison Terrence thought as she meandered purposefully through her grandfather's attic workshop. She loved exploring in the old attic because there were always new treasures to uncover, and discover.

Many specimens were geologic treasures that her father had received as birthday gifts. Jim Terrence always made a point to spend his entire birthday at home waiting for his gift to arrive, and he avoided work or anything else that threatened to take him away from the house on his special day. Madison always thought it was weird that her father seemed as sad on his birthdays as he seemed happy. But, that's grown-ups, she figured – they can be weird.

As she crossed the floor it creaked, partly from her weight, but mostly from the load of treasure that it bore.

The room bulged from floor to ceiling with a dizzying collection of the most awesome rocks, gems, minerals, and fossils anyone had ever seen. There were many pieces in the displays that even Madison couldn't put a name or mineral content on.

At eleven years old, Madison's knowledge of geology and other sciences had earned her the title of "youngest geology professor" ever to have taught at her hometown university in Cavern City, Virginia. Of course, she could only teach evenings and on Saturdays, because she had the fifth grade to deal with. But even with her vast knowledge of rocks and minerals, Grandpa Rocky's collection contained some specimens that she simply couldn't identify.

Madison disliked not knowing something. One matter she had recently begun to investigate regarded tales and accusations of her family's past involvement with something other-worldly and sinister. Her parents always brushed it off, which upset Madison. She couldn't understand why they never tried to defend themselves and the rest of the family. This stigma had taken a toll on her life, and she'd finally had enough. Wandering through the attic's vast shelves of treasures, she wondered if somehow the answer to the mystery might be right there under her nose.

Grandpa's Attic always smelled earthy, and at times a little musty. The aroma came partly from all of the old rocks and fossils. But mostly, the smell resulted from the room being completely underground. From the street, Terrence Hall looked like a two-story underground house, but it actually was a four-story house built into the side of a mountain. The bottom story was entirely below ground level like a basement, with no windows and only a back door. Grandpa's Attic was on the fourth floor, cut up into the mountain just above the bedrooms. The attic had no outside windows, so the only hint of the room's existence was a vent shaped like a bird house. This could be seen perched high on the cliff face, above the house.

The ceiling of the attic was high and domed. Rough and bumpy, it was the stone underside of the mountain the house was built into. When Grandpa decided to paint it to seal out the natural moisture, Madison suggested a night sky mural. Using glow-in-the-dark white paint for the stars was Mica's idea. At anytime, day or night, you could turn off the lights in Grandpa's Attic and gaze up at a starry sky.

"Cool! What's this?" Mica called out from high atop one of the bookcase ladders. In his outstretched hand was a small, rough-surfaced ball of rock.

"How did you get up here so quick?" Madison looked around for some clue as to how Mica had gotten to the attic before she did. She'd ridden up in the elevator, leaving Mica to climb the long carved spiral staircase.

"Magic!" Mica teased.

"If you're so smart, magic-boy, then you'd know that the object in your hand is a geode." Madison said. She tilted her head back slightly whenever she spoke in her educated tone.

She turned her attention to a huge microscope on a massive oak workbench. "Geodes form deep within the earth," she said, gazing through the eye pieces. "They begin with an empty space like a bubble in cooling lava or the empty space in the ground where tree roots used to be. That empty spot spends thousands of years being filled with layers of silica that cool and form crystals inside."

"Blah, blah, blah, yada, yada, yada," Mica groaned.

"Maddy is correct," Grandpa interrupted. "That's a geode."

"Listen to me, young one, and you are destined to learn something," Madison added. She crossed her arms and leaned back to rest her weight on one leg, her lips curled into a satisfied I-told-you-so smile.

"Let's crack it open to see if it has any crystals in it," pleaded Mica as he crinkled his nose to adjust his eye glasses.

Climbing down the ladder he started across the room, working his way toward Grandpa's workbench through a maze of wooden and glass display cases, bulging with geologic wonders. Mica rotated and examined the orb in his hand, imagining what might be hidden inside. He wasn't looking where he was going and bumped into a tall pedestal with a single object on it. The pedestal teetered back and forth, then... Crash! A beautiful stone box with an ornate gold latch fell to the floor and broke open. A huge clear quartz point rolled and bumped its way across the hardwood floor.

"Good one, Mica!" Madison admonished.

"I'm sorry, Grandpa." Mica said, ignoring his sister. At the moment of impact, he'd instinctively drawn his hands to his mouth and his apology muffled its way through his fingers. "I didn't mean to do it. It was an accident. I promise." Slowly he ran his hands up past his cheek bones and raked his fingers through his hair, stopping on top of his head with two hands full. Mica felt so terrible about what he'd done that he completely lost interest in whatever surprises the geode might have held.

"It's alright," Grandpa said. "Whatever it was, I'm sure I have more of them." His soothing voice made Mica feel a little better.

Grandpa spun his chair around to survey the damage and to assess the danger. He knew Mica was usually careful in the attic, so it must have been an accident. More importantly, Grandpa considered himself the supreme protector of these kids and he didn't want one of them upset about something as simple as a rock.

Mica bent down to clean up the mess he'd made. He examined the greenish blue stone box.

"The box and the lid are okay," Mica reported. Working the lid, he noticed that the hinges were okay, too, but the latch was just a little bent. "I can fix this."

He was very mechanical and fascinated with how things worked. When most kids got toys they played with them. When Mica got toys, he took them apart. He liked knowing how things worked. To him, nothing could be more fun. Naturally, Madison saw no value in this behavior because she thought it to be purely destructive. She could never understand why her parents tolerated it.

"No! Don't touch...." Grandpa called out. But before he could finish, Mica had already picked up the quartz crystal that had fallen out of the stone box and rolled under the edge of a display case.

"Ah, snap! This thing is warm." Mica held out the crystal in the palm of his open hand. "Creepy. It's getting warmer." He looked up from his hand and glanced toward his sister. "What?" he said, wondering why she looked like she'd seen a ghost, and was taking several careful steps backward.

"Galloping grape groundhogs!" Madison said. "Look at the floor. That's what!" Her voice had that high shrill quality produced when she was really mad, or really scared.

Mica cast a cautious gaze at his sister's feet and slowly moved his eyes back across the floor toward his own. The floor shifted and moved, like waves made by the wind cutting through a field of tall grass. The floor wriggled with snakes of all sizes and species, mingling together in a writhing viper soup. Frozen in terror, Mica released a scream that could not be expected from someone so small. Slowly, he started to sink into the deepening reptile quicksand. Afraid to move, he took a deep breath and held it as if slipping underwater.

Before his scream and its echo could fade, Mica felt himself moving through the air. Grandpa had wheeled in and scooped him up onto his lap.

"Now hand me that infernal thing," Grandpa said, "before you conjure up a dragon or something really dangerous."

Grandpa pried open Mica's white knuckled hand and plucked the quartz from it. With the crystal held toward the light, Grandpa squinted an eye and stared into it as if searching for something deep inside.

"Yikes! What is that thing, Grandpa?" Mica asked, trying to catch his breath.

"This is a piece of vision quartz," Grandpa replied. "It is very rare."

"I'll say it's rare," Madison added. "I've studied all of the rocks and minerals earth has to offer, and none of the books I've ever read mentions anything about vision quartz."

"I came across this piece many, many years ago, back in the days before…." Grandpa's voice trailed off. "Well, that was a long time ago. Anyway, when you hold this crystal in your hand it will show you whatever it is that you are most afraid of. Clearly, Mica, you are afraid of snakes."

"Give it to Maddy to hold," Mica begged. "I'll bet Jacin Means will show up right here. Maybe she'll get a whole bunch of Jacins." Mica knew that would get her fired up.

"You think maybe you've caused enough trouble for one day?" Madison was not in the mood to listen to Mica's childish foolishness, especially if it had anything to do with the one boy that taunted her at school and anywhere else he happened to see her. As she reached for the geode that Mica dropped before the snake invasion, Madison suddenly froze in place.

"Did you hear that?" she asked in a stern whisper. Stealthily, she turned toward the back of the room, her hand held up in a gesture for silence.

"Never mind the sound. What is that smell?" Mica whispered. He held one hand over his nose and mouth.

"Over there—by the bookcase ladder." Madison whispered. She motioned toward the ladder.

A strange scratching noise grew louder and she tip-toed slowly toward the source of the sound. Holding the neck of her pajama top up to cover her nose and mouth, she bent down out of sight of Mica and Grandpa. She was determined to discover what was making the noise and giving off a stench so thick it burned the lining of her nose.

"Digby!" Madison squealed. She popped up with a big brown fur ball of a rodent in her arms. "What are you doing? And Gees-Louise, what have you been eating?"

Digby, the pet gopher, had been with the Terrence family since long before Mica and Madison were born. Only Grandpa knew for sure how long he had been there. Digby spent most of his time with Grandpa in front of the television watching movies. Although generally an unnatural behavior for gophers, Digby loved watching movies and he seemed to understand what he saw. Over the years he and Grandpa had seen just about every movie that had ever been made. Many of them, especially the James Bond movies, they watched over and over again.

Anytime Digby wanted to go in and out of Grandpa's Attic, he made use of the vent shaft on top of the mountain. He'd dug an extensive tunnel system throughout the neighborhood that enabled him to travel underground, just about anywhere he wanted to go. Most of the neighbors didn't seem to mind. That is, of course, except for the next door neighbors, the Means family. Many times, Jacin Means had tried to catch Digby; but the little fur ball was always too smart to be caught. Digby seemed to be able to work things out in his head that an animal shouldn't be able to.

Digby squirmed to get down. Madison worried that, with the intestinal distress he had just demonstrated, she might require a change of clothes if she didn't promptly set him down. She stepped over to Grandpa's workbench and gently placed the tunnel rat amidst a pile of papers and rock collector's tools. The fluffy brown creature proceeded to pace back and forth, shifting papers around with every step on the expansive desktop. Digby leaned cautiously to his left and held up his right front paw. Then he returned his right paw to the table and lifted his left.

"Let's get him out of here before he explodes," Mica joked.

"I think he wants to tell us something," Grandpa said as he rolled to get a closer look at the dancing gopher. With his elbows perched on the arms of his wheelchair, Grandpa steepled his hands in front of his chin and tapped his fingertips together, one at a time. "Very strange indeed," he said.

The workbench was a massive wooden structure that dwarfed any teacher's desk the Terrence kids had ever seen. Digby, with his hugely rotund belly, looked really small when he sat on the desk. Burdened with tools and papers and numerous objects that Grandpa intended to catalog and put on display, the desk sat beside an unusually wide and strangely dark window, with a single light switch next to it.

Mica hopped up and pointed to the switch. He said, "Let's see the Grand Hall."

"Sure. Go ahead and cut it on," Grandpa said. He waved his hand in an upward motion. "I'm getting ready to go down there anyway, just as soon as I seal this vision quartz in my safe."

Click! With the flip of a switch, the once dark window

now revealed a brightly lit cavern. Orange, red and blue lights reflected their bright colors back through the window into Grandpa's Attic.

"The Grand Hall looks so awesome from up here."

Madison spoke without even realizing she had.

Standing before the window, the Terrence kids peered out over the most beautiful underground cavern they had ever seen. "It's like watching The Discovery Channel, only this is live," Mica declared.

"Ooh. There's my favorite speleothem!" Madison pointed to a cluster of cave coral down near the cavern floor.

"Speleo-what?" Mica twisted his neck to the right, so he could look at his sister when she delivered the answer. He lowered his chin and wrinkled his nose again from side to side, adjusting his glasses down a bit so he could peer over them.

Arms crossed in front of her, Madison glanced over her left shoulder and then down at Mica.

"Spel—e—o—them," she said slow enough for a preschooler to comprehend. "It just means 'cave formation.'"

"I suppose you couldn't just call it a cave formation, could you?" Mica asked.

Turning her attention back to the cavern, Madison tilted her head toward the calcium deposits of cave coral clustered together on the walls and said, "Like I was saying, there is my favorite speleothem."

"Looks like popcorn to me," Mica said.

"Cave coral is also known as 'cave popcorn,' because

that is exactly what it looks like," she added. "Just don't eat it. You won't have a tooth left in your head."

The kids shared a giggle, poking and laughing at each other. That didn't happen very often, because Mica was usually the one picking at his sister. Just as quickly as his smile had appeared, it drained from his face as he stared down at the pool in the center of the cavern floor. Madison turned back to the cavern below to see what had captured her brother's attention.

Rising in a pale bluish-pink mist above a stone pool of mineral water, a woman's shape appeared. She seemed to be a human, although a very small one. She stood only slightly taller than Mica, but she was definitely not a child. Her dress gathered tightly at the waist with gold braided rope. Her shimmering, pearlescent gown flowed out from the gilded braid and reflected sparkles around the room. Beautiful dark, curly hair framed her perfect face, pale except for a mild pink flush. She looked toward the Terrence children and seemed to plead with them. Desperately upset, the small woman's tears flowed like sparkling streams over her cheeks and down onto her gown, where they disappeared in its shimmer.

Motionless, Mica and Madison said nothing. They couldn't pull their eyes away from the image that hovered in the cavern. Unable to hear her, they could only wonder who she could be and what could be so urgent. Even more importantly, how did she get inside their cavern, and what she could possibly want with them?

"Last one to the Grand Hall is a rotten grape gopher," Grandpa called out as he rolled toward the elevator. "If you should get there first, you know to stay away from the water, right? Understood?"

"What? Huh?" Madison quickly re-gained her senses as the vision in the cavern dissolved. "Oh, uh, okay Grandpa." She wondered if she should tell Grandpa about the image. Being scientific-minded, she really wasn't sure if she believed what she'd seen. She remembered thinking that a stalker had loomed near the library, but that it had turned out only to be Jacin Means. So, Madison said nothing.

"Sure thing, Grandpa." Mica looked briefly up at his sister, then darted toward the stairs.

"Come on," Madison said, turning to Digby. Affectionately, she rubbed the underside of his chin with her fingertips.

Digby rose up on his back legs and reached for her. He had been sitting right beside Madison's newly repaired necklace, so she grabbed it and then scooped Digby up into her arms. Together they followed Mica down the beautifully carved spiral staircase that wound its way from Grandpa's Attic to the floor of the underground cavern.

6
The Intruder

In his determination to catch Digby, Jacin followed the gopher through the Terrence home's mountaintop vent shaft, and down into Grandpa's Attic. Digby scurried through the tunnel and crept out into the attic, but not before leaving behind something for Jacin to remember him by.

Jacin lurked quietly just inside the vent, afraid to come out until everyone was gone, but uncertain if he could stand to stay. The smell overwhelmed and smothered him. With a face as blue as the azurite minerals on the shelf just outside the vent, the suffocating intruder crawled out into the attic. Jacin had held his breath, avoiding the noxious vapor for as long as he could.

"If I get the chance, I'm gonna kill me a rodent!" Jacin called out across the attic. He rubbed his eyes to relieve the burning.

He stood up, and worked his way across the expansive room. Jacin's eyes watered and blurred as he surveyed the room filled with such wonders as he had never seen. He picked up gemstones, tossed around rocks, and ripped open boxes. He scraped his nails across the fossilized remains of some strange, ancient life. With a level of concentration that only Madison was known for, Jacin studied every piece, every specimen. He hoped to find evidence to prove that the Terrence family was connected with something evil.

"So this is the big secret of Terrence Mall—Wall—Hall—whatever," Jacin said. "More rocks. These people are *beyond* weird."

Jacin sifted through a tray of fluorite crystals. Selecting a large one, he held it up to the light. The pale purple stone revealed a swirling center that held Jacin's attention. He found it hard to look away. It was hypnotic. He closed his hand around the crystal, hiding it, to free his gaze.

"Cool," Jacin said.

He figured that with so much stuff in the attic, no one would miss one little stone. He pushed the gem into the depths of his jean pocket with long fingers, then retuned the tray to the table and rearranged the remaining stones to disguise his theft.

Moving from table to shelf, drawer to closet, Jacin went through Grandpa's collection like a Viking raiding a small village. Madison would have been furious if she'd known Jacin Means was in her Grandpa's attic touching the treasured collection with his filthy hands.

A tall black cabinet loomed in a corner. Its latched,

heavy door was an invitation for a boy like Jacin. He was sure the massive cabinet held a great treasure, since it required a lock. After prying the lock and pulling the door open, he stood in front of seven shelves filled with odd-looking figures carved out of different types of stone.

"Figurines!" Jacin blurted out in disappointment. "Who locks up stupid figurines?"

Disgusted, he leaned his shoulder against the great door and pushed. For a moment, he thought he saw movement through the disappearing crack just before the door closed. Certain he'd seen the elusive gopher, Jacin grabbed the handle and leaned back. He swung the door open and focused on the third shelf.

"Come on out you tunnel-digging varmint," Jacin demanded. "How'd you even get in there?"

But Digby wasn't there. Only figurines lined the shelf. Just as Jacin decided that his imagination was responsible for what he'd seen, a figure on the shelf in front of him winked. He bent closer to inspect the carving. On a white marble couch, etched with deep lines that created a plaid effect, six horned cat creatures sat, side by side, legs crossed and clawed paws folded across their laps. They seemed to be made of a slick gold-colored marble.

Unable to detect any signs of life in the strange cats-on-a-couch sculpture, Jacin decided to pick up one of the cats. It lifted easily from its place on the couch, and then came to life in Jacin's hand! The small beast waved an outstretched paw through the air above the others still sitting on the couch. Blinking and stretching, five more horned cats awoke.

The ferocious looking felines looked at each other,

and then pounced on Jacin like velociraptors on unsuspecting prey. With the fury of full size tigers, the tiny cat creatures pulled at Jacin's ears and ripped at his hair. They grabbed his shoe laces and knocked him off his feet. One nailed Jacin's shirt to the floor with its sharp claws, while above him two others struggled with a large piece of granite. They inched it toward the edge of the table, just above Jacin's head.

"Get off of me!" Jacin fought to get up off the floor, but he was kept busy fighting off the golden feline monsters.

The room began to take on a haunting green glow, and Jacin's eardrums vibrated with a low humming that filled the room. It reminded Jacin of submarine propulsion he'd heard in old war movies. Above his head, he watched as the sharp-edged, speckled rock inched farther and farther out past the edge of the table.

Just as the rock balanced itself above his head, suddenly the cats were gone. Poof! They just left. Jacin pulled himself free of the floor and sat up to look around. He thought they might have gone to get reinforcements. But there in the cabinet were all six horned cats sitting on their marble couch like nothing had happened.

Jacin jumped to his feet and slammed the cabinet shut. "This place is insane," he said as he panted for air.

He leaned back against the door to ensure that it stayed closed. While he took a moment to catch his breath, Jacin reached up and felt the cloth on his shoulder to see if he had really been nailed to the floor.

"Wicked!" He ran his fingers in and out of the claw punctures in his shirt. Then he noticed a strange orb across the room that must have cast the mysterious green glow. Its light flickered and faded out, and with it went the odd humming noise. Someone, or something, had tried to make contact inside the attic through the orb. Luckily for Jacin, it had frightened the cats.

Afraid to disturb anything else, Jacin carefully tiptoed to the window to see what it was Mica and Madison had been looking at. He peered down into the expansive underground chamber. Before Grandpa suffered the stroke that put him in the wheelchair, he had wired the cavern for electricity. The carefully chosen multi-colored light bulbs created a mystical, other-worldly atmosphere. Their light reflected off the damp cavern walls and shone through the attic window. Jacin felt the warmth of the glow on his face.

"An underground cavern?" Jacin wondered aloud. "This weirdo place is full of secrets I can't wait to tell."

Jacin wondered just how many secrets this unusual house held. He knew his father would be proud of him if he could discover the secrets hidden in the Terrence home. Jacin's father was never proud of him, and never offered him a kind word. Maybe, Jacin thought, this was his chance to show his father what he could really do, and finally win his approval.

Whatever might happen, Jacin knew he *had* to get down into that cavern.

7
The Krybosian Stairpath

Jacin crept down the staircase to the cavern floor level. He inched his way past the elevator door, then made his way out into the cavern where he found a thin formation tall enough for him to hide behind. He could hear Madison's voice. It sounded to Jacin like she was talking to a group of people. He leaned around and saw her pointing to a cluster of drippy cave rocks. She was talking alright, but there was no one else there.

"This is my absolute favorite," Madison instructed. "It is cave coral, also known as cave popcorn." She pointed to a bumpy rock cluster off to her right.

Madison practiced her cave tour presentation every day. Each semester, she and her parents invited geology students to the cavern. It was Madison who guided them around the Grand Hall, pointing out formations and answering questions. She knew every drippy stalactite that dangled from the ceiling of the main chamber. She knew every stalagmite, some short and some tall, that rose from the hard mud floor. The stalagmites seemed to strain upward, each reaching for stalactites to one day form solid floor-to-ceiling columns. Mica thought some of the stalagmites were creepy, and resembled other-worldly creatures. Some were almost human-looking.

"...four—five—oops!" Mica busied himself catching drops of pure spring water in his mouth as they slowly, rhythmically fell from the ceiling. His face dripped with crystal clear droplets that had missed their mark. The lenses of his glasses were completely obscured with moisture.

Both Mica and Madison kept a watchful eye on the pool in the middle of the cavern floor. Neither mentioned to the other that they'd seen the eerie human figure hovering above the pool earlier. But both were wondering if they would see it again, or if they had ever really seen it at all.

Grandpa maneuvered his wheelchair around the pool as if searching for something. Just then a bell began clanging. "Great galloping groundhogs!" Grandpa said. "Someone's at the door." He spun around and headed back inside.

"I'll be back," Grandpa added in his best *Terminator* impersonation. "Stay away from the pool while I'm gone."

Jacin watched as Madison stopped to stare at an empty wall. He shook his head disapprovingly as he thought to himself how little was required to entertain a member of the Terrence family. Jacin had never liked the Terrences, and now he was more determined than ever to learn their secrets and reveal them to the town, and particularly, to his father.

"That's interesting," Madison called to Mica. Slowly, she moved to the back wall for a better look.

"What's interesting?" he asked. "Rocks—in a cavern? Gosh, what'll they think of next? Water in the ocean?" Mica loved to jab.

"Don't be stupid," she replied. Her irritation with her brother's immaturity was evident. "Do you see anything different about this wall? Anything at all?"

"Maddy? You in here?" a voice called out with a beautifully rich South American accent. Onyx Ruiz entered the cavern looking for her American best friend.

"Hey, we're here, all the way in the back," Madison answered.

"Your grandfather let me in," Onyx said. "He's on the phone right now and said to tell you he'd be back down here in just a few minutes. He said for us to be sure to stay away from the pool."

"Gees, he's really been on that one all morning," said Mica.

After long awaited reunion hugs, Madison showed Onyx what she had been looking at before she arrived. "I was asking the immature one over there if he noticed anything different about this wall." Madison pointed to the back wall of the cavern, and then turned back to her brother for his answer.

"Okay, sis," Mica said, having decided to play along. "This part here looks like it's a different color than the rock around it." He rubbed his hand slowly along its slick surface.

"That's right. Different color, different texture, and there's an outline around it as well." Madison pointed toward the wall and traced a line in the air with her finger.

"Ouch!" Mica yelped. Drawing his hand back and clutching it in the other he said, "It shocked me. I've been rock-shocked!"

"Can't you be serious for one minute?" Madison asked. "I'm not playing games with you." She took the opportunity to point out that rocks themselves don't conduct electricity, although the water inside of them could.

"I am serious!" Mica demanded.

As Mica turned and held up his rapidly reddening hand as evidence, the oddly colored wall of rock behind him dissolved, revealing another chamber. It was a secret room filled with mist. The air was too thick inside to see how big the room was, or what dangers it might hold.

"Galloping gopher guts!" Onyx exclaimed. "We've got to investigate this." Stepping through the opening her eyes widened with excitement and anticipation. "I bet we're the first humans ever to walk here."

Digby followed without hesitation. He scurried past everyone's feet into the concentrated gray mist of the secret room. Madison, possessing an inquisitive and scientific mind like her best friend but without the same sense of adventure, was cautious to explore the new cave room. She leaned in behind Digby for a look.

"Maybe we should wait for Grandpa," Madison said. She glanced back to see if he had returned.

"Wow!" Onyx said, barely audible through a pinched nose and covered mouth. "This is *nasty.*"

"Sulfur, I suspect." Madison said, joining Onyx in the secret cave.

"It smells like really rotten eggs," Onyx answered. "So, yeah, it's either a pocket of sulfur gas, or Digby's stomach." Onyx was suddenly reminded of the last time she visited the Terrence home.

"Do you two really think I'm just gonna' walk, in my pajamas no less, into a strange cave room full of weird mist and gopher gas, after a morning of swimming in a sea of snakes, and after seeing a ghost lady in our pool?" Mica said. He plopped down on a rock bench, crossing his legs and then his arms. "Now who's being stupid?"

"*What* is he talking about?" Onyx asked.

"This entire day has been weird," Madison said. "I'll tell you later."

Watching from behind his pillar, Jacin's curiosity was peaked. He craned his neck around the formation that hid him, straining to see this secret chamber. Leaning a little too far, Jacin suddenly lost his footing on the slippery rocks and landed hard on his skinny backside.

"Oomph!" Jacin moaned.

He'd tried not to make a sound, but he had landed on a pile of broken, sharp-petaled gypsum flowers Madison had stacked there a few days earlier. Since these cave formations were broken and posed a tour hazard, she had moved them to a safer place where dripping water might allow them to continue forming. Madison would have been pleased to know they had caused Jacin Means some inconvenience, instead.

Jacin stood up fast and turned to inspect his backside. When he saw white crystal shards protruding from the back pockets of his jeans, he squinted his eyes so tightly he felt them pushing against his brain. He gritted his teeth, holding his breath and his bottom until the pain became bearable. Then, one by one, he plucked the strange, sharp flower petals from his behind and quietly laid them on the packed mud floor.

"Oh, it just keeps getting better. Check this out," Onyx called through the clearing mist to Madison and Mica. The thinning fog had lifted enough to allow better visibility. "It's a staircase!"

Mica leaned his head through the newly opened doorway to see what the girls had found. "Wow, guys. You've discovered steps," Mica said with disappointment. "Stairs, steps. Oooh, the excitement of it all."

"Yes. But where do they go?" Madison asked.

"Look at it," Onyx insisted. "Haven't you seen a spiral staircase like that before? I know I have, and I've only visited here a few times."

The look on Mica's face revealed he had made the connection between this mysterious staircase and the one he climbed everyday to Grandpa's Attic. Both staircases were made of a highly polished dark wood. Both handrails were intricately carved with strange vines and unusual creatures. Even the treads were the same, carved to resemble half-moon shaped lichens that grow on the sides of trees deep in the forest.

"But that staircase doesn't go *up*," Mica pointed out.

"Sure it does," Onyx said. "Just because it doesn't go up from here doesn't mean it can't go up from somewhere else. The question is *from where* does it go up?"

Digby began his descent down the newly found staircase. Mica noticed his familiar furry tail as it curved down the stairwell and out of sight.

"Galloping gopher grapes!" Mica screamed. "D-i-i-i-g—b-y-y-y!"

"We have to go get him," Madison said.

"Okay—but you first," Mica cautioned. "I'll be right behind you. I think."

Onyx stepped forward and began the descent. Very little, if anything, scared her. Her thirst for knowledge and the excitement of discovery drove her. Once, she was grounded for a whole month because she'd climbed down by herself into a new cave she'd come across in her native Peru. Her parents had been pleased with her discovery, but furious that Onyx didn't use the buddy system. She could have gotten into huge trouble, with no hope of getting help. Onyx rationalized since she had buddies on this trip, she was good to go!

"A little spongy, but I think it'll hold," Onyx said, planting a foot gently down onto the first step of the old stairs, half expecting it to collapse. Testing each step by gently bouncing on it, Onyx descended the staircase while calling to Digby and pleading with him to come back. Madison was only one step behind. Mica followed Madison, gripping the handrail so tightly that his red hand was turning white.

"You guys still there?" Onyx called out over her shoulder.

The mist had returned and she couldn't see a thing. No one could see anything, so no one noticed that Jacin had crept into the room as well, and was working his way down the staircase only a few steps behind them.

"We're here," Madison answered. "Any sign of Digby?"

"You're joking, right?" Onyx asked. "I can't even see the tip of my nose in this unnatural air muck."

The fog began to thin as the trio moved further down, revealing the staircase one step at a time. It began to look very different. The handrail was no longer made of wood with intricately carved vines. The treads were no longer carved wooden planks. This staircase was *alive*.

The stairs spiraled around a massive tree trunk. Real vines now curved around, down and out of sight, replacing the wooden handrail. The wooden stair treads were transformed into giant lichens attached to the side of the tree trunk, and arranged in a downward spiraling pattern.

"Are you seeing this?" Onyx asked, as she studied the structure all around her.

"I see it. I see it," Mica whispered. "Don't you think we should go back?"

"We can't—not without Digby," Madison insisted.

"And not without seeing where this leads to," Onyx added.

A powerful rumble began in the depths below and vibrated steadily up through the winding steps. The threesome clutched at the vine railing to keep from being knocked over. Then, without warning, the vines and lichens folded in. They smoothed over to form a spiral slide that swished the kids around and down, into the depths of the unknown.

8
Rocky's Return

As Madison, Mica and Onyx whirled into the depths of the earth down the living stairpath, Grandpa Rocky wheeled back into the cavern.

"Maddy? Mica? Your folks are on the phone," Grandpa's voice echoed through the empty cavern. "Come one guys. It's long distance."

He listened, but there was no reply. The only sound was that of rhythmic water droplets splashing onto the mud floor. Mica and Madison were gone. Even Onyx was nowhere to be seen.

It was obvious to Rocky that the kids hadn't entered the house since the phone was by the door and they would have passed right by him. He circled the pool in the center of the cavern as he looked for clues. Leaving the pool, he went directly to the back wall. There, he stopped.

Rocky saw fresh footprints pressed into the packed mud floor. They told him the kids had stopped to put their shoes on before entering the cavern. Not all rocks are smooth, and some are sharp enough to cut a bare foot quicker than an old pop top. That's why the family insisted on safety first. Mom and Dad had posted a sign and placed a rack of old shoes and boots at the entrance to the cave to remind everyone of the importance of sturdy shoes.

Mica and Madison's footprints, accompanied by a set of gopher tracks, traveled through the usual parts of the cavern, past the cave popcorn and over by the dripping spring. Onyx's footprints went straight to the back where they met up with the others. But strangely, all of the footprints stopped at the back wall of the cavern. It was as if the kids had walked right through the solid rock wall. Rocky rolled away from the wall and leaned forward in his chair to study the tracks, contemplating the danger that the coming days would hold.

"So it begins again," he said. Grandpa leaned forward, resting his elbows on the arms of his chair. One at a time, he tapped his fingertips methodically together in front of his face. For years, he'd known this day would come. He'd planned for it, but he never thought it would happen without him.

Why hadn't he told the kids more? He wondered. They knew so little of what lay ahead. Rocky wished he'd been in the cavern when the portal opened up. At least then he could have guided and protected them.

And he *would* have been with them, if it hadn't been for that phone ringing. The phone! He'd forgotten that his son, Jim, was on the phone waiting to talk to his kids. He'd have to come up with something to tell him, until he could get the kids back.

"Uh—Jim?" Rocky spoke into the phone, pausing briefly for a response. Then, he added, "Onyx has already arrived and the kids are busy chasing down Digby, and you know how that goes. It may be a while before I can get them to the phone." Rocky didn't approve of telling lies, but he'd been known to put a half-nelson on the truth for a good cause. His son had important work to do out west, and Rocky figured he could handle the situation here with the kids. Once he had his son convinced everything was under control, Rocky rolled into the elevator and started for his attic.

"Come on, come on!" The elevator seemed especially slow to Rocky today, or maybe it just seemed that way because he was in such a desperate hurry. Rocky nervously tapped the arms of his wheelchair while he waited for the door to open into his attic. As the lift squeaked to a stop on the fourth floor, Rocky popped a wheelchair whee-lie that Mica would have been proud of, and one that Madison would have been completely embarrassed for Onyx to have seen. He rolled out of the lift even before the doors had a chance to completely open.

When Rocky discovered that Mica and Madison were missing—along with their summer visitor, Onyx Ruiz—he knew what had happened, and what he had to do. He opened his safe and pushed aside the vision quartz that had caused Mica so much trouble earlier. From the depths of the antique iron box he removed a tattered bundle, rolled up and lashed with a leather cord.

He laid it on his desk and carefully untied and then unrolled the soft brown suede, until its contents were revealed. Rocky picked up the eight-inch-long, spike-shaped crystal. The top looked like a beautiful round diamond with a flat head. The spike itself had a sharp stabbing tip that Rocky took care to gently lower into his shirt pocket. Last summer, when Mica first saw it, he said it looked like a stake meant for a vampire's heart.

"Well, I suppose I'm as ready as I'll ever be." Rocky locked the safe, then moved quickly over to the orb that had filled the room with color and sound during Jacin's attack. He placed one hand on the side of the orb, then closed his eyes and waited. Motionless, Rocky looked more like he was sleeping than in a big hurry. From under his weathered hand, white sparks flowed down toward the orb's center, seemingly into dead space. He waited.

The orb began to hum. An eerie green light burst from its center. When it reached the outer shell, light exploded into the air, illuminating the entire room. Green streaks of light escaped past Rocky's fingers to create an otherworldly effect on his face.

"Hello, my lady," Rocky said. His face lit with teenage excitement.

"Do you know what's happened?" Queen Marcelene asked.

"I know. I've seen the signs that I feared for a couple of days now, but I didn't want to believe it." Rocky removed his hand from the orb and cradled it on his lap with the other. "This time, the grandchildren are caught right in the middle of it."

"Our furry friend will bring them to the castle where

they'll be safe until you can get here," Queen Marcelene said. "But please, please hurry. Mourgla is at it again, and now with all three of the Ashclaw pieces here in Krybos, he may succeed."

Marcelene's pleas tore at Rocky's heart. He was worried for the kids, and for the people of Marcelene's world, Krybos. He rolled a few feet back from the orb so the woman could see his wheelchair. He laughed and said since stairs were out of the question, he'd be coming through the pool portal. She nodded in agreement as the orb's glow faded to black.

Grandpa took some comfort from the fact that his grandchildren hadn't entered that portal alone. Digby's tracks were right alongside the children's. He knew they couldn't be in better hands—or paws. What did worry him was the extra set of oversized human footprints that had followed the children through the portal.

9
A New Land

After a wild ride down the vegetation slide, Mica, Madison, and Onyx found themselves face down on the ground in a strange meadow. All around them stood the bare stalks of spindly, tall plants. Above them loomed a thick canopy of sprawling green leaves that seemed to appreciate the constant warmth that enveloped the land. Streams of light punched through and pounded the ground all around. Only a few yards away, they heard crunching, munching, and then delighted moaning.

"Somebody—*do* something!" Mica whispered. "I don't know what that is, but it sounds hungry and it's coming this way."

Onyx motioned for everyone to lie still while she sat up to peek above the layer of leaves that hid them. She gazed across the open meadow, focusing her concentration on the area where the strange sounds came from.

Not ten feet away from where they had landed Onyx saw the creature with May apples in each paw, and its cheeks bulging with the sweet fruit. She reached down and tugged at Madison's pajama collar, slowly pulling her up so she could peer out over the leaves.

"No, Digby! Those are poisonous!" Madison screamed as she sprang to her feet.

Digby sat in the center of the field of May apples, eating them as fast as he could. His fur glistened, soaked with the sticky juice that dripped from his mouth.

"Nawt heyaw, they're nawt," Digby said in a strong Scottish sounding accent, reminiscent of Sean Connery's.

"James Bond?" Mica stood up to see for himself, startled by Digby's suave accent.

"By the way, Miss Maddy, the name is Amon Ossian Zollicoffer," Digby said. "But, you can call me Digby. Rocky gave me that nickname years ago and I rather like it, seeing as how I spend a great deal of time digging."

"You talk?" Madison asked.

"Of course I do—well, here anyway. Let me welcome you all to Krybos," Digby said, holding his sticky paws up to the sky to present his world to his human friends. "I'll answer any questions you might have, but we really must get moving. Mourgla will know we are here, so we must get to the safety of the Step Castle as quickly as we can. That means you too, Jacin." Digby called out across the field. "You can't stay here."

"Jacin? Jacin who?" Madison spun around in horror. She hated being harassed by Jacin Means, and she hated even more being harassed *about* him.

She turned and saw a figure rise up out of the May apples to stand taller than all of them. It was Jacin.

"Oh my freakin' gosh!" Madison was sick. "What are the odds? It's mathematically impossible!"

She could hardly believe it. She had miraculously traveled to an entirely new world deep inside the earth, and somehow, Jacin Means was there. What rotten luck! She wouldn't have minded if anyone else had followed, but not the one person in the whole world who made her stomach churn every time he came near.

"What is this place?" Jacin asked. He demanded to know how their secret room and staircase had put them there. "You guys are going to be in a world of trouble when we get back!" Jacin pointed at Madison, then at Mica. "You too!" he said, glaring at Onyx.

"And what makes you so sure *you'll* be getting back?" Digby asked.

"Yeah, and what makes you think we know anything about the stairs, anyway?" Mica added. "It's the first time I've ever seen them."

"Just wait until everyone hears about your grandfather's attic full of creepy stuff, and the secret stairs, and this fat furry talking rodent," Jacin announced.

"You've been in the attic?" Madison exclaimed. "*My* Grandpa's Attic?" She dropped her head, then began pacing and mumbling to herself.

"Oh man, I sure hope you didn't touch anything," added Mica, actually hoping that he had.

"I tried to tell you, Maddy dear, that he'd followed me and was hiding in the vent shaft," Digby said. "Unfortunately, when I'm in your world I can't speak. I can only do what gophers do. And in that vein, I must apologize for the foul odor. The clover has been especially flavorful this year."

"I've seen enough and I'm going back now. Where is that stupid staircase?" Jacin demanded. He stomped around aimlessly in the field, trampling Digby's favorite fruit.

"Pipe down over there, Jacin. Do you want Mourgla to find us?" Digby said. "Oh, and mind who you are calling a rodent. If my memory serves, and it always does, you spent the morning crawling through underground tunnels yourself."

Digby tried to explain their situation, but he wasn't sure the kids were ready to believe how extraordinary it was.

"That stupid staircase you refer to, Jacin, is not an ordinary staircase," Digby said. "It's a stairpath, a portal between your world and mine. You and I don't have any control over when it opens, but there are those who do. One such person is Queen Marcelene, who lives in the Step Castle in the city of Elea. We have to reach her before Mourgla finds us. She will help us."

Digby turned and started across the May apple meadow, motioning for everyone to follow him as they began their journey to Elea.

"Who is Mourgla?" Onyx asked as she followed in Digby's path.

"I have a feeling it's a name we'll wish we'd never heard," Madison replied.

10
The Eyes of Krybos Are Watching

On the other side of Krybos, deep inside the dark fortress of Demelza, the evil Mourgla awaited his victims. He walked to a massive stone table that had a recessed top filled with fluid. The surface shimmered with a thin layer of the glowing substance. Peering into the luminescent liquid, he briefly pondered his reflection, the visage of a disfigured monster he kept hidden beneath a hooded robe. As his reflection faded, a view from the Krybosian landscape took its place.

"Welcome, surface dwellers," Mourgla said, his breath moving the shroud he wore to cover his face. He delighted as the images in the water table revealed that his plan was proceeding right on track.

Mourgla watched the new arrivals as they walked through the bright green field. He needed the piece of chalcedony that Madison wore around her neck, and soon it would be his. The two extra children that came through the portal were of no concern to him at the moment, but getting Digby back was a treat he could only have dreamed of.

"That's right, Digby. Lead them to the Step Castle." Mourgla's deep voice sent chills throughout anyone unlucky enough to hear him. "Ah, my little friend, how wonderful it is that you've returned to your world." He drummed his nails on the edge of the table, creating vibrations that rippled across its fluid surface, blurring the images with each distinct tap.

Mourgla was still very angry with Digby for helping Rocky Terrence and Queen Marcelene prevent his take-over of Krybos. The excitement within him swelled as he thought of how he would finally be able to pay Digby back for meddling fifty years ago.

As happy as he was to have this chance to get revenge, Mourgla also knew that Digby would warn the children about him, and about the dangers Krybos held for the uninitiated. Mourgla *had* to get to them first. He sum-moned his stealthy cat patrol and sank into his massive green marble chair, to await their arrival.

"But who is this *other* human, the skinny one?" a sheepish voice asked.

It was Jacaa, Mourgla's assistant, posing the question. He wasn't a great assistant, but Mourgla never had much luck finding help that was competent and also willing to be subjected to the steady ridicule and strife that was life in the dark and cold fortress of Demelza. Jacaa, at least, was willing. He lowered his head and cast a cautious gaze up at Mourgla to see if the question had angered him. He hoped it hadn't.

"What other human?" Mourgla said as he pushed Jacaa aside.

"That—uh—tall boy," Jacaa said as he tried to steady his ancient frame. As far as anyone in Krybos knew, Jacaa was the oldest inhabitant of the interior world. His round face was etched with deep wrinkles and framed with thick white hair, from the top of his head to the beard on his chin. He preferred to keep his face hidden beneath a hood, not because he felt ugly, but because the hood and shroud served as a barrier between him and Mourgla. Better still, Jacaa thought, when Mourgla made him mad or gave him an awful task, he could fire off a few obnoxious facial gestures, without Mourgla or those irritating cats seeing him do it.

As Mourgla gazed into the water table, he saw the boy's image in the gently rocking water. It was the tall thin boy from Cavern City, but now he was in Krybos, standing at the edge of the May apple meadow.

"That's interesting," Jacaa said. He asked, "Why does this one not follow the others?"

"Interesting indeed," Mourgla said. "I've seen this boy in the surface world. His interference caused me to miss getting the last piece of the Ashclaw crystal. One thing's for sure, he's not a friend of the Terrence family. Perhaps we can persuade this one to help us out with our little project."

Two of Mourgla's horned cats clamored into the room and bowed at his feet. Their golden fur was ruffled and littered with small pebbles and dust. Each tried to brush the other off before Mourgla could notice, but behind them, a trail of filth tracked with paw prints betrayed them.

"I can only assume there was a terrible explosion in the kitty litter storage, and you two were unfortunately caught in it," Mourgla said, as his anger became apparent.

"Well, no. See…," Lucian started to speak.

"Actually, it's like this," Scratchley said, picking up Lucian's explanation. "We were just.…"

"Silence!" Mourgla interrupted. He held one hand up to stop another nonsensical attack on his ears.

Despite their shortcomings, Lucian and Scratchley were Mourgla's favorites because they would do anything he asked of them. They weren't the smartest cats in their litter, so sometimes they got into trouble. Lucian's left horn had a small chip in it where he had tangled with a fanged lizard over a snacking mouse. Scratchley's tail was bent at the tip where he'd closed it up in a door.

Mourgla motioned Lucian and Scratchley over to the water table and showed them the image of the tall young boy all alone in the meadow. They leapt up onto the edge of the table and watched as Jacin walked out of the meadow, and entered the forest. Mourgla ordered that the boy be caught and brought to Demelza, emphasizing that the boy was not to be hurt. Mourgla needed to win Jacin's trust if he was going to be able to use him.

Suddenly the image blurred, as deep waves rippled across the surface of the table. Jacaa quickly reached up and snatched Scratchley's bent tail out of the water, then threw his hands behind his back hoping to go unnoticed.

Jacaa passed one foot gracefully back and forth in front of himself, bowing his head in a display of innocence.

"Why do I surround myself with such incompetence?" Mourgla bellowed as he motioned for everyone to leave.

Tumbling from the table to the stone floor, the two horned cats landed on top of each other with a painful *thud*. Then quickly, they scrambled to their feet and raced each other out of the room, eager to please their boss.

As Lucian and Scratchley hurried out of the dark fortress of Demelza to set a trap for Jacin, Digby and his friends pressed on toward Elea, hoping to stay out of sight and avoid Mourgla and his evil horde.

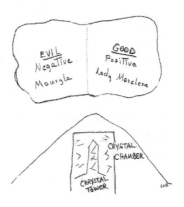

11
In The Balance

"So who is this Mourgla?" Madison asked, as she marveled at the strange new world surrounding her. The green May apple meadow gave way to wooded hills that reminded her of southwestern Virginia, except for some odd plant life and the weird luminescence that hung overhead.

"Mourgla is an evil man who wants all of Krybos for himself," Digby replied. "Many years ago he tried to kill our world by making Krybos uninhabitable. We would all surely have died, had it not been for your grandfather."

"So what good would this place be to Mourgla, if it was uninhabitable?" Onyx reasoned. "He wouldn't be able to live here either, right?"

Digby stopped suddenly and turned to face the kids. "Sit, just for a moment, and let me tell you the events of those many years ago," he said.

Digby scuttled behind a rotting log and emerged to

perch on top of it. "Do any of you recall hearing about a big earthquake that hit the center of the United States, about fifty years ago?"

"I'm very familiar with it," Madison said. "Earthquakes are unusual for that area of the country."

"That's right," Digby replied. "Very unusual."

He went on to explain the events leading up to that earthquake. "Krybos is divided into two halves. Mourgla is pure negative energy, and lives in one of the halves. Marcelene is pure positive energy, and lives in the other. Anytime either is on the surface world, it causes disruptions in that world. Fifty years ago, Mourgla was there. He was preparing a place for himself and his helpers to stay while they waited for Krybos to collapse and die. That big earthquake was a sign that Mourgla was in the surface world. Once Krybos was dead, Mourgla planned to return and correct the imbalance he had created. Then with Krybos restored, Mourgla would found a new order there and he would be sole ruler of *both* sides."

"Okay, I don't like this guy at all!" Mica said, taking his glasses off and wiping his forearm across his face.

Digby continued. "Krybos is held constant by the earth's magnetic field, and any reversal of this magnetic field can destroy the delicate balance that keeps Krybos alive. Any natural shifts in the earth's polarization can be dealt with if we know they are coming, but less so with deliberate attempts to alter it."

Digby told of a wondrous place with a crystal tower, located within a Crystal Chamber deep inside the purple mountain of Zaltana. The kids listened with excitement and disbelief. Madison tried to recall everything she had ever read on magnetic fields. Onyx imagined what fun they'd have adventuring deep inside a purple mountain. Mica tried to work out in his head what the mechanics of a crystal tower included, and wondered what it would be like to take it apart.

"It's all pretty simple," Digby explained. "The crystal tower controls the earth's rotation and its magnetic field. Fifty years ago, Mourgla entered that chamber deep inside Zaltana and reset the tower. From the moment that the final adjustment was made to the tower's crystals, the clock was ticking and all life in Krybos depended on stopping Mourgla, and restoring the crystal tower to its original state."

"And where does Grandpa play into this?" Madison asked.

Digby continued, "Your grandfather was working in the quarry near your house on the day Mourgla got into the Crystal Chamber. Rocky was digging so close to an opening in our world, that many at the Step Castle were able to watch him with remote viewing. That's a gift of sight that most Krybosians have, but few surface dwellers are able to use. If you can harness it, you can see people and places in your mind without having to go there."

Mica looked at Madison and smiled. They both knew very well about this remarkable mental gift.

"Anyway," Digby said, "the people of Krybos watched Rocky work everyday, and were fascinated by this man who worked with rocks. Marcelene could tell that he was a good man, so she came to him at the quarry and asked for his help in stopping Mourgla. That was the day that water flooded the main pit of the quarry. It's that balance thing, you know. When a Krybosian comes to the surface world, there are consequences. When a surface dweller comes to Krybos, there are consequences."

"Uh oh. What will our being here cause?" Madison was trying to understand the strange concept.

"As it happens, the bigger the surface dweller, the bigger the consequences," Digby said. "Children are generally too small to cause a major problem so we should be fine, at least for a while."

"I'll bet *he* can find a way to cause one," Madison knuckled Mica lightly on the shoulder.

"Well. I'm not the one who can't get from the school to the town library without gettin' into trouble and needing a rescue crew," Mica said.

"Ouch!" Onyx said, hearing the sharp, verbal jab Mica just made at Madison and clutching at her heart as though it had been pierced with an arrow, then giggling at her friend.

Madison realized a point had been made and joined in the laughter. When she turned her attention back to Digby, he was laughing and struggling to get back to his story.

"To make a long story short," Digby continued, "your Grandpa Rocky agreed to help. He shut down the quarry, then came here and saved our world."

"Cool!" Mica said. Pride beamed from behind his eye glasses.

"Rocky came here to help?" Onyx asked.

"Of course he did. There's nobody like Rocky," Digby said.

"Wait a minute." Madison suddenly remembered

something. She looked as if she'd just been given a bad grade on one of her tests. "There *has* been unusual earthquake activity in Arizona during the past few weeks. That's where Mom, Dad, and Onyx's parents are right now."

"Has there been anything else unusual?" Digby asked. "Anything at all?"

"Well, there's the birds," Mica noted. "We saw a blue jay that couldn't fly in a straight line the other day, and the next morning the song birds couldn't even sing. They sounded horrible."

"It seems as though Mourgla has recently been in Arizona, and in Cavern City as well," Digby said, proud as if he had just solved a complicated puzzle. "Obviously, we were not lured here by accident. Mourgla *knows* we are here."

The furry gopher turned, dropped off of the log and disappeared out of sight. "Let's go, quickly," Digby said, peeking around the end of the log and motioning for the trek to resume. "We must reach the Step Castle by nightfall. We don't want to be outside at night, in Krybos."

12
Crossing Krybos

The foursome walked until they came upon a cliff draped with stringy sheets of pungent, green moss. The musty layers dangled like icicles on a winter tree, obscuring the rock face they had overtaken. With deft paws, Digby patted the moss-covered cliff. He lifted its strands and looked behind each one until he finally found what he was searching for.

"Stay close and don't lose me," Digby said.

Mica grabbed onto his sister's ponytail in preparation.

With one quick leap, Digby pounced through the moss and disappeared. The kids looked first at each other, and then back at the mossy tangle. Just then, a furry paw poked its way out and beckoned to them. Madison hoped Digby knew where he was going. Onyx didn't care as long as Digby took them on an interesting adventure to an unknown place.

The kids counted off: one, two, three, and pushed their way through. The tight tangle of moss gave way to an open area, a tunnel with dirt-caked tree roots dangling from the ceiling. The roots wiggled and shifted in and out of the kids' path, shedding dried cakes and clods of dirt as they moved. Digby scurried ahead on all fours, well under the layer of dangling roots.

"Stay down low, away from the roots," Digby called out. "They are as alive as the plants above that they feed, and they are constantly searching for nourishment. If they find you, they will wrap around you and make you into a cocoon, and here you will stay until you are completely consumed."

"Cocoon—consumed," Madison whispered. She looked over her shoulder at Mica to be sure that he understood the danger.

He did. Mica was short for his age and probably wouldn't have had to crawl on all fours to stay out of the reach of the roots, but he did anyway. Like a parade of babies, the kids crawled single file through the dark tunnel, trying to keep up with an overanxious gopher who was obviously trying to get home.

After what seemed like an hour, the tunnel finally opened up onto a high, rocky ledge that overlooked a beautiful green valley. At the bottom, a shimmering, dark river meandered through the center of a lush oasis. This deep valley had protection on all sides by high mountain walls equally rich in vegetation. Digby led the way down a steep trail that dropped into the valley below.

"Now be careful, because… ," Digby's voice trailed off.

He shouted the warning over his shoulder to the procession following close behind. But before he could complete his sentence he disappeared, barreling down the mountainside in an uncontrolled roll toward the bottom.

"Because why? I wonder," Mica asked. "And where'd he go in such a hurry, anyway?"

"I think he meant *be careful* because you might slip," Onyx said. She tried not to laugh, but she couldn't hold back.

Onyx's face lost all expression as the crumbly soil beneath her feet suddenly fell away. In a flash, she, too, was gone. Mica and Madison could hear her voice all the way down the mountain side, whooping and hollering like she was on a water park slide. Before either could say anything, they found themselves hurtling down the slope behind Onyx, on their way to the valley below. Madison led the way with Mica behind her, holding onto her ponytail like a rope on a snow sled.

The group was reunited on the valley floor, deposited on a small blue beach where the mountain slide had sent them. Everyone stood up and brushed away the dirt, leaves, and twigs from their clothes and hair. Digby shook his fur like a dog after a soaking bath, and then congratulated everyone for making the trip—or slip—unhurt.

Madison didn't listen. She was too busy sifting the brilliant blue sand through her fingers, trying to determine its origin. Onyx dropped to one knee and ran her hand across the beach, leaving a wavy design where her fingers had passed.

"I've seen white sand, tan sand, and black sand, but never blue sand," Onyx said.

"Blue sand—me neither," Madison said. "Of all the blue crystals found on earth, none occur in such large deposits that they could break down over time like quartz does to create a sandy beach."

"Awesome!" Mica said. "We *have* to take some back with us."

Mica scooped a handful and offered it to Onyx to store in one of her pockets since she was the only one not wearing pajamas.

Digby ambled over to the edge of the river. He stared into it for a few minutes, and then turned to address the kids.

"We are looking for a place where the river runs backward," Digby said. He stretched a paw out toward the water. "It's somewhere downstream from here. Just keep an eye out for water that looks like it is moving the wrong way, upstream."

They followed the river's edge, studying the swirl of the water's flow. The current moved steadily, licking its way around boulders and downed trees. Wherever it flowed over submerged obstacles, the water smoothed out on the surface. Swirling eddies formed in various places along the river's edge.

"Does this river have a name?" Onyx asked.

"Yes," Digby said reluctantly, but added nothing more.

"Are you going to tell us what it is?" Mica asked.

"Now don't be alarmed, or read any more into this than necessary," Digby cautioned. "But, it turns out that this river is called the River of Death."

"Have a lot of people died in it?" Mica stepped to the edge and cast his gaze across the water. He hoped to catch a glimpse of whatever had given the river its name. All at once he was knocked off balance as a hand grabbed his shoulder, pulling him firmly back a few steps.

"I don't like it," Madison said. She let go of her brother and turned to Digby. "Why are we looking for a section of the river that flows backward?"

"We must find it to get safely across this river," Digby said. "The Step Castle is beyond this river and there is only one way to cross without the risk of dying in this water."

Mica grabbed a handful of leaves and threw them into the river. He figured he could watch them float downstream, twisting and turning on the water's surface with every change in the current. All they had to do, Mica reasoned, was watch for the leaves to start moving back upstream. But just as Mica dropped the leaves, the river began to boil violently from its depths, rumbling like a big pot of spaghetti cooking on high heat.

Before he could scoop up a second hand full, Digby firmly grabbed Mica's wrist. Then he put himself between the kids and the river. Standing on his hind legs and facing the water, Digby stretched out his arms in front of them as they all moved back from the riverbank. Slowly he inched himself and the children away from the river. The water would return to normal before Digby dared to move again.

"You keep *that* up and we'll all get to see why this is called the River of Death," Digby said in a quiet, nervous voice.

"Do you mind telling us *what,* exactly, that was?" Madison asked.

"Snakeheads," whispered Digby.

"You mean snakehead fish like those found in Asia?" Onyx chimed in. "How is it that you have surface world fish living here?"

"The snakehead fish was introduced to the surface world many years ago, but it is really a native of Krybos." Digby corrected Onyx. "The only difference is that, on the surface, the fish are fairly tame. It has something to do with your aquatic environment."

Madison had heard enough. "I don't know what you've been reading, but snakehead fish are not tame on the surface world either. They are toothy predators with voracious appetites that have been seen launching themselves out of the water to reach their prey. They have an unnatural intelligence, and acute visual and olfactory senses, and they are destroying every ecosystem they invade. Tame? I don't think so."

He appreciated Madison's academic approach to things she'd studied, but life in Krybos was not something you learned from a book, Digby thought. Actually, it was not something that had ever been written in a book.

"Maddy. Dear, sweet Maddy." Digby looked up at her as he spoke. "Trust me when I say *tame*. You take your surface world snakehead menace and multiply that by 1000, then you can start to get an idea of how terrible the snakehead is in its native environment."

"Okay, that's not good," Madison said.

While Mica and Madison were getting the snakehead lecture, Onyx had wandered along the river bank studying the water and pondering the terror it held. Suddenly she stopped and called to the others.

"Hey, it's here!" she said, pointing to an area where water flowed around both sides of a large boulder and swirled back up stream behind it.

Digby shuffled over to confirm the spot. Then from the river's edge, he instructed everyone to do exactly as he did. Turning toward the river, he picked up a small polished pebble with orange streaks and tossed it into the backward flow.

"Be sure that your pebble goes into the backward flowing section," Digby said, pointing to where he had landed his rock.

Within seconds, the water bubbled gently beside Digby as a gigantic water lily gurgled to the surface, and opened. With water streaming off of its ivory petals, it extended one onto the river bank, forming a bridge from the land over into the heart of the flower.

Digby stepped onto the long petal and walked across, where he took his place in the center. Quietly, he reminded everyone to do *exactly* as he had done, one at a time. Then, the flower closed around him and sank beneath the surface. Everyone waited to see what would happen, but there was nothing more to see. Digby was gone.

"How well do you trust a gopher that talks like a movie star and who, before today, no one even knew *could* talk?" Onyx asked.

The Terrence children looked at each other and smiled. "With our lives," Madison and Mica spoke in unison.

Mica bent and picked up another polished stone with orange streaks, and stepped lightly over to the edge of the river. Under his sister's watchful eye, he repeated Digby's moves and also disappeared into a flower. Choosing a stone for herself and one for her friend, Madison placed the rock in Onyx's hand.

"Do you want to go first?" Madison asked.

"You go ahead and catch up with Mica." Onyx said. She wasn't afraid to be last, so she insisted her friend go ahead. "I'll be right behind you."

"Okay. I'll be waiting for you—wherever this ends up," Madison said. She tossed her pebble, stepped into her waiting lily, and disappeared beneath the surface of the river, swallowed by a flower.

Onyx stepped to the river's edge and repeated the process. Then she, too, descended into the unknown depths of the River of Death. Afterward, the river returned to its original peaceful appearance, leaving no indication that they kids had even been there.

Beneath the river's surface, the giant river lilies followed an old established network and transported the children, not just across the river, but to a place further downstream. At the end of the journey, the flowers erupted one at a time from the water and spit out Mica, Madison, and Onyx a safe distance away from the river bank. A soft pad of hexagonally-shaped mushrooms proliferated and provided a perfect pad for landing.

"Where've you been?" Digby asked, pleased that everyone had made the trip alright.

"Don't you have boats, or cars, or normal ways of getting around?" Mica asked.

"Normal for where?" Digby responded. "For *your* world or for *mine*?" He stretched one paw toward a pink and purple crystalline castle that stood tall amid a dense cluster of mineralized stone-clad houses, located at the bottom of yet another, and even deeper, valley.

Rising toward the sky, its highest points reached nearly to the top of the valley walls. The Step Castle got its name because of its stair-step design. Five smaller yet distinct structures, each resembling the main building, were carved into and clinging onto the valley walls. Arranged in a well-spaced and circular pattern, together these smaller buildings resembled a staircase to the valley floor. The structures seemed to spiraled around and down toward the largest section of the castle, positioned centrally at the bottom.

Elevated and arched stone bridges stretched from structure to structure down the valley walls, connecting the castle buildings and creating their unique spiral shape. The final bridge arched high over the main castle's tall protective stone wall and entered the shimmering crystal palace itself. This main part of the castle situated on the valley floor was enveloped by a beautiful garden, and both were well protected behind the high stone wall.

"That is the city of Elea," Digby proudly announced. "And down there, at the center, is the Step Castle. We'll rest safely tonight."

13
Jacin and the Horned Cats

Lucian and Scratchley tracked Jacin throughout the night. Fortunately for them, this task was made easier because Jacin carried in his pocket a multi-function crystal that he'd taken from Rocky Terrence's attic treasure room. Among other things, it was a locator crystal. Without it, the two bumbling, bungling cats would have never found anyone but each other. That would have displeased Mourgla, and was something they tried never to do.

Jacin had spent his first night in Krybos alone in the woods. As the eerie Krybosian daylight began to overtake the night glow, Jacin slept as his stalkers encroached upon him. Hungry and scared, Jacin had taken cover the previous night under a rotten, moss covered log. It was here that he still slept. Because of the density of the forest, Lucian and Scratchley found it difficult to get an exact location on Jacin, but they could smell him.

The horned cats circled in a confused pattern until they decided exactly which log contained the sleeping boy. Scratchley set up a trap, just a few feet from the log that hid Jacin. Now all they had to do was lure him out into the open, and their nets could scoop him up.

"I bet he's hungry," Lucian said, wiggling his ragged ear. "Let's put some food out in the open and then wait for him to come out." Lucian prided himself on great ideas.

The two felines scoured about until one of them found a carreby. It was a small furless squirrel-type creature with wrinkled pink skin and drooping hound dog ears. Although not much bigger than a snacking mouse, it would have to do. They breathed their foul breath on the carreby, and it went limp in Scratchley's paw. He placed the animal on open ground, then followed Lucian to the tree tops to wait for Jacin to take the bait. And there they would wait. And wait.

"Maybe humans don't care for carreby," Scratchley pondered.

"Maybe. Humans are pretty weird." Lucian replied.

After a long while, Jacin poked his head out as he heard the carreby start to wiggle and rustle in the leaves upon which it lay. When curiosity had finally gotten the best of him, Jacin came out to see what was wrong with the little creature.

"Curiosity kills the cat, but it gets the human captured," Lucian hissed.

Together, Lucian and Scratchley dove from their perches high above Jacin, pulling their nets down with them. They landed with a thud that surprised Jacin.

Startled, he jumped aside and took a stance like an under-fed sumo wrestler, ready to engage his competition.

"Oh, this is another fine mess you've gotten us into," Lucian sneered from underneath the net meant for Jacin.

"Me? This was your lame idea!" Scratchley was trying to get out from beneath his own net.

Jacin thought the two strange creatures were trying to catch the carreby. He laughed at the incompetence and misfortune of these two forest animals that couldn't even catch their tiny meal. "You guys are pitiful, " he said.

Lucian and Scratchley grew angry at Jacin's laughter. The sound of sharp, feline talons unsheathing echoed through the forest. Suddenly, Lucian remembered Mourgla saying the boy must not be hurt. If that happened, Mourgla would surely kill them when they returned.

"Put those away, now. *Nice* kitty." Lucian said, patting the back of Scratchley's hand. He had calmed down and retracted his own claws and was trying to convince his fellow feline to do the same.

"What a side show you two are," Jacin said. He was still laughing at the two clumsy cats as he pulled away the nets that ensnared them. It was then that he noticed their horns and realized he now faced the same monstrous creatures that had so savagely attacked him in the Terrence family's creepy attic.

"Oh, snap!" He turned to run, but before his feet could carry him away he was scooped up in the same nets he had just helped the vicious cats to escape from.

"Thanks for your help, human," Lucian sneered as he tied off his rope.

He and Scratchley each grabbed a line, and together they began to pull Jacin across the bumpy forest floor, all the way back to Demelza to be presented to Mourgla.

Jacaa stood guard at the door to Mourgla's lair, waiting for the horned cats to return with their quarry. When Lucian and Scratchley arrived with Jacin in tow, Jacaa ushered them into Mourgla's main dining hall where a huge table awaited, piled high with sweet-smelling breads, fruits, and roasted meats of all kinds.

"We intend you no harm, boy," Jacaa said. He motioned for the cats to release Jacin from the netting. As Jacin stood up, brushing the dirt from his pants, Jacaa continued, "In fact, we want to help you."

"What makes you think I need any help?" Jacin asked.

Jacin leaned against the wall by the door, fidgeting with the crystal in his pocket. Nervous, he shifted his weight from one leg to the other, back and forth.

"You did spend the night alone in the Krybosian woods, and most of today in a net, did you not?" a deep, gurgling voice inquired as it moved past him and into the room.

A dark figure loomed its way to the table at the center of the room. Turning to Jacin, the shadowy form threw back an oversized hood and misty shroud to reveal its hideous face. Covered with pale, translucent flakes of skin and netted with an array of surface veins, the man's face made Jacin look away on sight. Odd lumps and misshapen growths crowded Mourgla's features and took the place of hair on his bare head.

The last time Jacin had seen this face, it was hovering just behind Madison on the sidewalk in front of the Cavern City library. Such a hideous sight it was, the face haunted his dreams that night. And now here it was right in front of him, looking at him, talking to him. Jacin slid a hand down the back of his neck to calm the rising hairs.

"I am Mourgla," the ghastly figure said. Raising one hand, he waived everyone out. Then, looking Jacin in the eye, he clarified, "Everyone except you, of course. We have business, Mr.—?"

"Means. My name is Jacin Means." Jacin tried steadying his voice to disguise his nervousness, but he wasn't having much luck. "Hey, I've seen you with Madison back in Cavern City. Are you her uncle or something?"

"I was not *with* the young Terrence girl, nor am I related to her," Mourgla announced. He moved along the side of the table toward a tall, ornately carved seat at the other end. "I was trying to retrieve something she has that belongs to me. That's when you showed up."

"So you're *not* one of her weird relatives?" Jacin commented. "You sure could have fooled me."

"Please, help yourself," Mourgla said. He lifted his outstretched arms to present the feast. He was trying to control his dislike for the boy's foolishness and planned to deal with him later when his usefulness came to an end. Mourgla pointed to Jacin's skinny frame and added, "You look as though you are starving."

Jacin was indeed hungry. He was tall and skinny, but

it was not for lack of eating. He had a very fast metabolism which burned off everything he ate. As Jacin placed a hand over his empty stomach, it rumbled in response. His initial reluctance and fear suddenly seemed like minor matters in comparison to his desire to eat.

As Jacin began to fill himself, Mourgla asked him how well he knew the Terrence family. Jacin, not surprised by this question, replied that he knew them, all of them, in fact.

"I hate them," Jacin mumbled through a mouthful of food. "And I hate their stupid gopher. I followed them down the stairpath so I could find a way to ruin them."

Dragging a long, sharp fingernail through red dipping sauce and slowly drawing it out, Mourgla shook the last loose drop off and ran the nail across his tongue. With an evil kind of joy on his face, Mourgla said, "Jacin, you've come to the right place for destroying the Terrence family."

With a smear of creamy potatoes on his face and barbeque sauce dripping from his chin, Jacin offered an uneasy smile. He suddenly didn't feel so frightened in this strange new world. In fact, he was certain he was going to fit in just fine.

By the time Jacin had his fill at the table, he'd heard Mourgla's plan and agreed to do his part in helping to destroy the Terrence family. However, he was a little unsure of having to work along side Lucian and Scratchley.

"Now let me get this straight," Jacin said, leaning forward to rest his elbows on the table. "I am supposed to work with these two creatures?" He looked directly at Lucian and Scratchley.

The horned cats each sat on a cushion in a far corner of the room. Lucian was struggling with a mammoth fur ball he couldn't seem to hack up, while Scratchley licked and chewed at a burr caught in the fur on his back, tantalizingly just out of reach. They stopped their activities briefly to scowl and hiss at the very suggestion that they would be difficult to work with.

Mourgla assured Jacin that, if the cats messed up, he would see to it that they were at the next feast, as one of the dishes. Jacaa glanced at the two cats, snickering over their potential misfortune. Anytime Mourgla rode someone else's back, Jacaa was delighted. His snickering stopped abruptly when Mourgla looked his way, clarifying that the "feast fate" would befall *anyone* in his service who messed up.

Stuffed and happy, Jacin pushed back from the table and stood. His rotund belly protruded so noticeably from his thin frame that he looked like he had swallowed a basketball. Taking their cue from Mourgla, Lucian and Scratchley pounced toward the door of the hall, nearly knocking Jacaa off his feet.

"Mangy, flea-bitten…," Jacaa's voiced trailed off when he noticed Mourgla was staring at him. Suddenly realizing his hood was off, Jacaa made eye contact with Mourgla and then petted Lucian sharply on the head. "Nice kitty," he added with a half-hearted smile.

Hsssst. Lucian hissed and faked a claw-packed swipe toward Jacaa.

Jacin followed the felines into the interior of the lair where they prepared for their assigned task. With their plan in place, Jacin and the horned cats began their journey loaded with netting and ropes meant for capturing Digby and Madison, and anyone else that got in their way. Jacin was told to be certain he returned with the last piece of the Ashclaw Crystal and Madison. If at all possible, he was to capture Digby, as well. Mourgla had special plans for that meddling little beast. Jacin was determined to win Mourgla's approval by returning with at least the crystal, Madison, and the rodent. But he figured capturing anyone else would be a bonus.

Mourgla had said that Madison and the missing piece of the crystal could be found in the Step Castle, located in the center of Elea. Jacin and the two fumbling felines spent the afternoon working their way across Krybos and through the dark forest that bordered Elea.

Hiding just inside the fringe of the forest, Jacin waited there for most of the day. Mourgla had said that Queen Marcelene would already have instructed the kids not to leave the safety of the castle grounds. Jacin would have to trick them to draw them out, and he knew just how to do it.

14
The Castle at Elea

Light burned through the window of the Step Castle. Unlike the streaming sunlight Madison usually saw on her own bedroom floor each morning, this light glowed strong, oozing into every place it could find. It didn't appear to emanate from one particular source. Rather, it seemed to come from everywhere overhead and it blanketed the sky, the ground, and the entire city. The outside of the castle glistened with its coating of pink and purple crystals. The walls and towers twinkled so intensely in the Krybosian light that they appeared as if they were being consumed in a blaze of fire. It's the sort of scene Madison would have found breathtaking had she been awake to see it.

"Get up!" Digby shouted. "There is much that I want to show you before you return home." Digby ripped the covers off of the pedestal bed and scurried down to the floor with Madison's blankets trailing behind him.

"Digby!" Madison scolded. She clamored to retrieve her luxurious bedding but had reacted too late. She caught a glimpse of it disappearing over the edge of the bed. Madison raked her knuckles across her eyes, wiggling and twisting them to sweep away the night.

"Girl, this is no time to sleep," Mica said. His head popped over the edge of the bed to greet his sister. "Come on, Maddy. This is the most awesome place and you're sleeping right through it. Get up!"

"What in the name of all things sacred are you wearing?" She asked, peering down over the edge of the bed as her brother climbed down its ladder.

"This is the uniform of the castle guard—without the weapons, of course." Mica dropped to his feet from the last rung and sprang back up doing a half-turn to the left and then to the right, so his sister could admire his new outfit. "I've been named an honorary guard!"

The soft, royal blue top looked like a jacket embellished with shiny gold accents on the cuffs, collar, shoulders, and on the bottom edge. The pants were of the same comfortable material, with shiny stripes down the sides of each leg and around the cuffs.

"Here's something for you to wear," Digby pointed to the clothing hung on the stairs of the bed. "So, get up and get dressed. We're off to wake Onyx, and then we'll be waiting for you downstairs in the *Jumanji* Room."

Mica and Digby raced out into the hall, laughing and poking at each other. Madison wasn't sure what a "*Jumanji* Room" was, but she was sure that Digby and her brother would find some trouble to get into so she'd better get up and keep an eye on them.

Madison climbed down the bed's golden ladder, and walked over to lock the huge slate doors to her room. She leaned back, taking a moment to study the room. It was a palace-sized round room, with a high glass ceiling. Its floors and walls shone with polished marble blocks. She could hear herself breathing as the sound echoed off of every hard surface. The windows were built tall and wide to allow the glowing light of Krybos to freely enter.

Positioned in the center of the room, the bed was built up on a high marble pedestal with layer after layer of padding that reached half way to the ceiling. The golden ladder was the only route to the top of the bed.

"How did I ever get up there?" she asked herself. She was so tired when Digby got them to the Step Castle the evening prior that she didn't remember the room, or even how she climbed the ladder.

The bed was so incredibly soft that Madison felt she had spent the night in the clouds. Nice bed that it was, she was kind of glad that she didn't have one like it at home, or else she'd be sleeping away her valuable reading time.

Looking around the room, Madison noticed no other furniture. No dressers, no nightstands, not even a dressing table with a mirror. Nothing - except that bed. Then she noticed that the walls had decorative gold handles on some of its marble blocks. When she pulled on one, a drawer opened to reveal a collection of books. Another held brushes and combs, new toothbrush and soap. A third drawer contained old documents and pictures. She reached in and picked up a stack of photographs.

Sorting through them she came across a picture of her grandfather, as a younger man, at some kind of outdoor gathering. *Grandpa really was here!* Madison thought, as she studied the strange world in the background of the photo. He stood on a platform beside a beautiful woman—the same small woman whose image had hovered over the pool in the cavern. In the image, Grandpa was shaking hands with a little man hoisting a trophy. High above them, against the backdrop of the eerie Krybosian sky, hung a banner proclaiming *Memory Olympics Champion.* Madison thought to herself how much she'd like to participate in an event like that.

Finally, proof! Madison thought. There it was in this one photo of her Grandpa, the strange world she'd heard about for years, and a gathering of super-intelligent people. She decided that no one would mind her hanging onto just one picture. It was a picture of her Grandpa, after all, so she kept it out, then smoothly slid the drawer closed.

Madison gently traced a fingertip over the woman's face, wondering if this might be Marcelene. She thought about Grandpa's connection with this queen and her world called Krybos. She also wondered about her own connection with this world. Certainly, the secrets of her family's mystery were here. She knew the only way she would get any answers would be to go out into the castle to find them. She tucked the picture into the waist of her pajamas and patted it as if it were a small child needing comfort at bedtime.

Madison spent only a few minutes in the bathroom and then came out to get dressed. Lifting the clothes Digby left for her and holding them up for inspection, Madison smiled with approval. The peach colored shirt was smooth and shiny as silk and felt cool to her skin. She slipped it on over her head and the smell of flowers filled her nose as she pulled the shirt down into place.

Nice pants, too, she thought. They were just like her favorite jeans, dark and perfect with no fading and no rips. Even the shoes were cool like the hiking boots she'd begged to get for her last birthday. Everything was exactly the right size! *How strange*, she thought. Checking her reflection on the shiny marble wall, Madison pushed a few stray strands of hair into place. Carefully transferring her photographic evidence from her pajamas to the back pocket of the new jeans, she was ready to meet her destiny.

Madison pried open her bedroom door to reveal a moving walkway that continued the entire length of the hall. It disappeared from sight as it followed the curve of the hall. The mechanized walkway featured a split in the middle and was divided just like a road, with traffic on the right side flowing one direction and traffic on the left flowing the other. Signs at every intersection provided directions to different areas of the castle. In front of each door, the walkway had a flat turntable built in.

Madison stepped out into the hall and onto the moving circle in front of her door. She stayed on it until it rotated her away from the door and over to the balcony side of the hall. When properly lined up in the direction she'd decided to go, she stepped off of the turntable and onto the moving sidewalk. She wasn't sure where it would take her but she was excited to find out. She could hear Mica squealing with delight as he and Digby rode all around the castle on the moving sidewalks. As she continued down the hall, a door opened and Onyx leaned out.

"You've got to try this," Madison said. She motioned for Onyx to jump on board.

Together they rode the hallways of the Step Castle. Each connecting hallway had a rotating turntable in the walkway directly in front of it. Whether a person wanted to go up or down a hall, or to come out of a room and choose to go left or right, the turntable would line him up in the right direction. The trick was stepping off at the right time.

The girls marveled at the wondrous beauty of the castle, investigating every hallway, every room. The halls were alive with the diminutive citizens of Elea running errands and going about their daily life in the castle. Caught up in the grandeur, they quickly forgot they were supposed to meet up with Digby and Mica in the *Jumanji* room. By the time they remembered, they realized that they were lost. Madison could hear her brother giggling somewhere down one of the halls, but the sound of his voice echoed off the marble walls and made it impossible to tell which hall the voice had come from.

"Follow me, dear," a soft voice spoke from behind.

Madison and Onyx turned to catch a glimpse of a small woman in a blue gown, gliding down one of the halls. Madison thought this might be the same woman she'd seen in her cavern and in the picture with Grandpa. She wondered if it could be Queen Marcelene.

Madison and Onyx tried to catch up, but the walkway only moved at one speed. The figure in the blue gown was moving away as fast as they were moving toward her. The distance between them would never shorten. They would have to run. Running on an already moving walkway was like nothing the girls had ever experienced. They felt like they possessed the speed of Olympic track stars.

When they finally got close enough to see the woman approaching the end of a brightly lit hall, Madison noticed a gopher prancing around at her feet.

"Digby, wait for us!" she called.

The gopher abruptly turned to address the girls.

"I'd hardly consider myself to be even remotely similar to the creature you call Digby." The indignant gopher spoke firmly, making it clear that she could not possibly be "Digby."

"You're a girl!" Onyx said with surprise.

"My name is Chessa" the gopher replied. "And before you ask, yes, I know who Digby is. The insensitive scoundrel left here many years ago and never bothered to say goodbye, or even to come back to see if we were okay after that incident at the Crystal Chamber. We thought he was dead, but later learned that he was only dead to us. He was alive and well and living in the surface world."

"I'm sure he would have come back if he could have." Madison tried to ease Chessa's apparent anger.

Chessa lifted her nose to the air, turned, and followed the blue-clad woman into a large jungle room filled with trees and plants of every imaginable size and color. The perfumed smell of exotic plants and flowers permeated the air and enveloped everyone who entered. Madison and Onyx peered past Chessa and the woman to behold an amazing sight. The room before them housed a multi-story living jungle.

The girls proceeded into what could only be the *Jumanji* Room.

15
Castle Tour

Droplets hung heavy on the high domed ceiling of the *Jumanji* Room. A translucent coating of moisture made it look like the roof of a greenhouse. The air throughout swirled with the perfume from multiple varieties of flowers that bloomed near the floor. Somewhere in the thick foliage, Digby and Mica could be heard frolicking in a game of hide and seek.

"Welcome to Elea," a small, but stately figure pronounced as she turned to address her guests.

It *was* the woman in the photo with Grandpa Rocky. It was the same woman who had appeared above the pool in the Terrence's cavern. She looked at Madison as she spoke.

"My name is Marcelene. There is no need for you to introduce yourself, Miss Maddy Terrence, since I know very well who Rocky's grandchildren are."

The handsome monarch reached out and took Madison's hands in hers. Holding them tightly, she seemed to be as much in awe of Madison, as Madison was of her. Suddenly, Madison felt an incredible energy running throughout her body and withdrew her hands in fear.

"What kind of magic is that?" Madison asked, as she rubbed her tingling hands.

"Magic? No, there's no magic here, dear." Marcelene replied. "Just because something is different than you are used to, doesn't necessarily mean there is magic behind it."

"Well, that certainly *was* different."

Turning her attention to Onyx, Marcelene said, "This young lady I've seen in your cavern once or twice, so I know she is a friend. Any friend of the Terrence family is a friend of Krybos."

"This is my best friend, Onyx Ruiz," Madison said, reaching over to put her arm around Onyx. "She is staying with me this summer while our parents are in Arizona."

Cracking branches and rustling leaves caught Chessa's attention, prompting her to leave Marcelene's side to spy on whomever or whatever might be the source of such a horrible ruckus. Chessa crept into the thickly forested center of the room then climbed one of the few tall, but sparsely leafed, trees. Inching her way out onto a branch, Chessa stopped where she could sit just above Mica.

Mica was on his knees with his head stuck inside a gopher hole, yelling for his companion to come out. As he reached in and grabbed onto Digby's feet, and began to pull him out, Chessa slipped to dangle from her perch overhead. Her sudden squeal caught Mica's attention. When he looked up, he saw the gopher suspended from the tree overhead.

"Oh gees, Digs!" Mica exclaimed. He quickly realized, if that was Digby in the tree overhead, then the feet he had a grasp on belonged to someone, or something, else entirely! When Mica turned loose of the mysterious creature in the hole, it made a painful crashing sound as it hurtled into the back wall of its hiding place.

Mica reached up and helped the dangling gopher to safety. Chessa's kind and proper thanks made him realize that she was indeed not Digby and, in that case, he must have let his old friend smash into the back of the hole when he turned him loose. Mica set Chessa down on the ground and knelt by the entrance to the hole. He shouted apologies into the tunnel, and pleaded with Digby to come out.

"Let him stay in there," Chessa snipped. "It's not like anyone here is going to miss him."

"Uh oh," Digby said. He peered out at Mica, rubbing at the fresh lump on his head. "Did that voice belong to a gopher – say, about so tall and with massive dark eyelashes?" Digby indicated height by holding up a paw, and pretty eyelashes by batting his eyes.

"I'm more of a gopher than you'll ever be," Chessa said. "I don't abandon my friends." She crossed her paws in front of her in a display of disgust.

"You have to let me explain," Digby begged, crawling out of the hole on his knees. "I've had fifty years to come up with an explanation that wouldn't make you mad, but all I have to offer you is the truth—if you're willing to hear it."

Digby possessed an adventurous heart, and all his years in Krybos were spent longing for the intrigue and discovery found in the surface world. This passion had led him up the spiral staircase with Rocky fifty years ago, but it was his love for the Terrence family that kept him up there for so long. Digby had always intended to come back to Krybos, but put it off for fear of the reception he would get upon returning. His fears were completely realized in the present moment.

"Very well, I'll meet you in the *Temple of Doom* Dining Hall," Chessa said. She turned to disappear through the doorway.

"*Temple of Doom* Dining Hall?" Mica asked. Having seen enough of Grandpa's and Digby's favorite movies, he knew an *Indiana Jones* reference when he heard one.

Marcelene had been watching the exchange between Digby and Chessa, and then came over to the children to explain. She told them that the Step Castle was a refuge and home for the citizens of Krybos, and she allowed them to decide how it should be decorated.

"The 'movie theme' idea began in the center of the castle in our community room where a surface world signal freely enters Krybos," Marcelene said. "There, movies that play in the surface world can be viewed on a very large set of crystals. Over time, the citizens of Krybos developed a fascination for surface world movies and their characters. So, our rooms look like scenes from different movies. I'm sure you'll recognize them as you explore the castle."

"So your garden room looks like a jungle scene from the movie *Jumanji,* and your dining hall looks like a scene from *Indiana Jones and the Temple of Doom.*" Mica said. "That's too cool—I want to see more!"

"Remember this," warned the queen. "You may tour the castle and the grounds, meet and enjoy the people of the Step Castle, but do not venture beyond the walls surrounding the castle grounds. I have spoken with Rocky and he is on his way to get the three of you and return you safely home."

"He's coming all the way here to get us?" Madison asked.

"Yes," Marcelene said. "And until his arrival, you must avoid Mourgla, the most evil man in Krybos. Mourgla is trying to reassemble the Ashclaw Crystal."

"Fifty years ago Rocky broke the Ashclaw Crystal into three pieces and dispersed them to different locations," Digby said as he scampered out the door to meet Chessa.

"That's right," Marcelene said. "But Mourgla has already managed to acquire two of the three pieces. That means your arrival here is no accident." She pointed to Madison and continued, "That necklace you wear contains the third piece. If Mourgla gets all three pieces, he can reset the tower that controls the earth's rotation and magnetic field, and our fates, just as he tried before. You and the crystal will be safe as long as you remain here at the castle."

"Hey! I just figured out where I've seen you."Mica said excitedly. "You were in our cavern."

"Yes, child," Marcelene replied. "I tried to warn your

family, but I didn't want to come to you in person since my presence would have caused a disruption in your world. That's why I only appeared in your cavern as an image. Maybe if I'd have taken the chance I could've prevented all of this."

"Wait a minute," Onyx said. "If this Mourgla reverses the earth's magnetic field, won't that also cause problems in our world, the surface world?"

"Probably not," Madison replied. "Geologic evidence found in the rock of our spreading sea floors shows that the earth's magnetic field has previously shifted during the history of the earth. However, it is interesting to note that no shifts have occurred since humans have been on the earth."

"Great." Mica added.

Marcelene sent the kids to meet up with Digby and Chessa in the dining hall. After a visit to the *Men in Black* Game Room, the *Finding Nemo* Aquarium Room, and every other movie-themed room in the castle, the tour proceeded outside to the *Secret Garden* gardens.

Chessa, still angry with Digby, was on a quest to outdo him on the sightseeing tour. She led the kids down to the Script Stream, a remarkable ribbon of water that reacted to whatever came in contact with it. Currents that moved across the surface of the blue-green water would spell out names, or sometimes, warnings.

"Cool, huh?" Chessa said, shaking her finger dry as her name appeared in the water.

"Any snakeheads?" Mica asked.

"No, it's okay," Chessa replied. "Go ahead and give it a try."

Mica reached in and instantly his name rippled across the waves. He cheered with excitement when his name swirled across the surface. Onyx dipped her hand, then stood back and watched as her name boiled to the surface.

"Wow!" she said in amazement. "We don't have anything like that in Peru."

"Your turn, Maddy," Mica said. "It's *really* warm."

"All of the rivers and stream in our world are warm," Digby said. "The water is heated by the magma in the earth, you know, like the water that shoots of your Yellowstone Park geysers. We even have one stream that is so hot you can't touch it, or you'll be seriously burned. We're fairly certain nothing lives in that one."

"What are you afraid of, sis?" Mica asked. "Try it."

"I did try it!" Madison said, holding up wet fingers as evidence. The water boiled and churned in a wild and confused manner, hinting at an odd assortment of letters and symbols, but refused to give up her name.

"Okay, that was weird," Chessa said, resting a paw on her furry chin.

"Let's move on." Digby led the kids to the bird sanctuary.

He whistled a strange call and a blue-headed wood chipper quickly flew in and perched on his head. Then Digby whistled a few notes prompting the bird to dart to the tree tops, where it immediately began chipping away at a branch. A few moments later, the bird returned carrying a hollow branch lined with freshly drilled holes, and placed it at Digby's feet.

"Go ahead, Mica," Digby said. "Pick it up and play something."

Mica gently lifted the branch to his lips. As he forced air into the woody flute, beautiful music poured out of it. Onyx and Madison were very surprised at the quality of the music, but not as surprised as Mica was. He had never had any musical training, but now he played like a professional. The sound just flowed on it's own with no skill required, only air.

"It's magic!" Mica said.

"No, not magic," Chessa replied. "Things that may seem magical in your world are just normal here." Chessa replied.

Digby placed a paw to his mouth and whispered, "Listen."

"I hear it, too," Onyx added. "It sounds like someone is crying beyond the wall, in that thicket of shrubs." Onyx pointed to an area of heavy brush just through the wall's heavy gate.

As they neared the gate, they heard cries for help and realized they had forgotten about Jacin.

"Great gophers!" she said. Even though she couldn't stand that boy for the horrible treatment she'd suffered at his hands, Madison knew it wasn't right to leave him alone in a strange world with no one to help him. "We've got to do something."

"I suppose we should," Onyx agreed.

"No way!" Digby said. "Even if I did like that boy, which I don't, we must stay inside the castle grounds. Just wait here. I'll go to Marcelene and see if she'll send the castle guard. Don't go anywhere. I'll be right back."

As Digby scampered back to the castle, the cries grew louder and more intense but then died out completely. The kids listened but heard nothing but silence.

"I think he's dead now," Mica said. "I guess there's nothing more to worry about, unless Jacin is Madison's secret love."

Madison's genuine concern for Jacin's safety allowed her to overlook yet another one of her brother's attempts to make her mad. She *had* to see what was going on, whether anyone went with her, or not.

"I'm going to see if he's alright," Madison said. "It's the right thing to do."

She crept beyond the gate, drawing closer to the spot from which the final cries had come. Onyx was close on her heels, followed by Mica whose curiosity had won him over. A little further back, Chessa inched her way along with them. She lagged behind, hoping to give Digby time to return with the castle guard.

"It was right about here, I think," Madison reached to pull a tangle of brush aside.

Suddenly, a bony hand emerged and latched onto hers. Jacin had set a trap, and she'd gotten pulled right into it!

"Grab on, guys," Onyx yelled as she grabbed Madison's ponytail.

Mica grabbed onto Onyx and leaned back. Two long ruts trailed where he'd dug his heels in for traction. Chessa jumped in and grabbed Mica by the ankle. But even together, they were no match for Jacin and the two horned cats. With a final hefty tug, Madison, Onyx, Mica, and Chessa disappeared into the thick brushy trap, headed for an unknown fate.

16
Captured

Jacin led his quarry single file away from the Step Castle and back to Mourgla's lair, with each captive tied to the one ahead with a heavy rope. Meanwhile, Digby was bounding across the castle grounds, hardly able to contain his excitement. He had gone back to get the castle guard, but returned with Rocky Terrence, himself.

"Look who's here!" Digby called out.

But, no one answered.

"Mica? Maddy?" Rocky called out, but no one answered.

"Onyx? Chessa? Are you out here?" Digby shouted. His face wore a look of concern that couldn't be hidden, despite his fur.

Digby led Rocky over to the edge of the woods and pointed out where he had last seen everyone. He pointed to where the cries had come from, and where he had told the children to wait. Digby scurried back and forth, sniffing the ground for any clue. He'd hoped they had gone back inside the castle, but he knew better. Their trail ended at a thick clump of brush just at the edge of the woods, beyond the castle.

"It's no use, Digs. They're gone," Rocky said, his voice desperate as he considered what lay ahead of them.

Rocky knew the kids were in great danger. Marcelene had told him that Madison still wore the crystal when she last saw her. That meant Mourgla had now achieved the means to reset the crystal tower housed deep within the Mountain of Zaltana. He could reverse the earth's magnetic field, so that the north pole would become the south pole, and the south would become the north, and the destruction would begin.

Fifty years before, Rocky arrived just as the conditions in Krybos were reaching a critical point, with little time remaining to reset the tower. With the strength of a younger man, Rocky faced the formidable challenge and managed to save Krybos. But now, fifty years and one wheelchair later, Rocky doubted that he could repeat the feat. Help would have to come from somewhere else, but he didn't know where.

One thing he knew for certain, Mica, Madison, and Onyx were in great danger and he intended to find and rescue them from the clutches of that horrible creature, Mourgla.

Turning to Digby, he said, "You know this means that Mourgla has all three pieces of the Ashclaw Crystal, don't you?"

"Yes. Quite a revolting development, indeed," Digby replied.

Rocky reached into his shirt pocket and removed the sensing spike he had retrieved from his attic safe. He passed it to Digby who inserted it into the ground. Then Rocky instructed Digby to see if he could locate the kids, and Chessa.

Planted in the ground, the sensing spike radiated electrical 'feelers' just under the surface. It emitted continuous waves that traveled through the ground for miles which then returned to display images and sounds on its head. Like seismic echo location, the spike could detect any life form on the surface of the ground under which the waves flowed. With a few twists for adjustment, Digby rotated the spike to clear the reception.

"Nice," he said.

"Have you located them?" Rocky asked.

Leaning over the arm of his chair to view the images coming in on the spike, Rocky noticed that Digby had tuned into a girl gopher sleepover, just getting underway up in the castle.

"Amon Ossian… ," Rocky's voice trailed off as Digby tried a few more adjustments to the spike's tuning. He always used Digby's real name when he wanted to show disapproval.

"Oh, sorry—seem to be having a little trouble here," Digby said. "There, I think I've got it now."

With a final turn of the spike, Rocky and Digby saw Jacin and his two horned cohorts leading the kids and Chessa into the dark mountain fortress of Demelza. With finer tuning, Rocky and Digby were able to follow the group's progress through the creepy lair as they were taken to meet Mourgla. Rocky and Digby watched, listened, and learned.

The forest of Demelza was dark and cold. Its thick trees and brush prevented light from entering and made passage very difficult, especially for someone dragging a rope and several other people.

"Do ya' think you could lift that rope just a little higher?" Madison asked Mica, as she picked herself up off of the forest floor, and shook her ponytail to clear the twigs and leaves.

"I'm trying to hold it over my head now!" Mica snapped.

Mica was tied behind his sister in the captive procession. So, when his short stature caused his section of rope to tangle in the brush, the person walking in front of him would be jerked to an abrupt halt. This usually involved Madison getting yanked backward, and off her feet.

"Here, I'll help you out," Onyx said. She was always ready to help, having already decided to carry Chessa.

With the rope freed, Mica rode piggy-back on Onyx, with Chessa squeezed comfortably between them, and both looking over Onyx's shoulder. The ominous journey through the dark forest soon brought them to Mourgla's lair at Demelza.

The towering and imposing structure, constructed of dark, unevenly cut stone blocks, stood singularly in a clearing. Mourgla's lair was so tall that it reached beyond the hovering cloud-like mist that choked the towers of Demelza's main structure. A strange shine lit the stone surfaces to reveal man-made chips, much like the edges of a flint arrowhead. This shine came not from the stones being polished, but from a dampness that the surrounding forest had wrapped about the structure. Moss had crawled its way from the edge of the forest over to the building, and had started to overtake its walls. Two massive statues of evil-looking horned cats stood guard on each side of a small wooden door.

"We're back!" Lucian called out as he bounded toward the building.

Scratchley raced ahead and pushed open the front door to the main hall.

"Thrilled, I'm sure," Jacaa said. He met them at the door with a smile, but his demeanor revealed no joy.

Jacin led his captives inside. Still tied to each other, the children and Chessa followed Jacaa down a poorly-lit hall where he motioned for them to step onto an old platform. It was an open lift, like an elevator, but much more dangerous because it had no sides or door to keep its passengers on board. The gap between the edge of the lift and the floor was big enough for someone to fall through.

"All aboard," Jacaa said. "I just love saying that."

He turned to see that he was the only one amused. Clearing his throat and raising his arms to shake them free of his sleeves, Jacaa reached high and tugged on the ancient pulley system. Creaking and moaning, the platform started its rise through the dark interior of the structure. The elevator seemed to growl in agony as it climbed past countless levels until, with another tug on the pulley, it scraped to a stop on the highest floor. Here, on both sides of the hall, were only rooms with bars instead of doors.

"Not good, guys," Onyx noted.

When he hopped from the elevator, Jacaa landed on the slick cobbled floor and his feet slipped out from under him.

"Yeow!" Jacaa screamed. He quickly balanced himself to avoided busting his backside.

"I'd give that at least an 8," Jacin said. He always found it wildly amusing to laugh at other's troubles.

Jacaa glared back, but said nothing because he sensed that Mourgla stood, watching, just beyond the shadows. "Come on—all of you," he said.

"Let's go at the same time and balance each other," Onyx suggested to Mica.

Together, they leapt from the elevator and when they landed, they slipped across the floor ending up standing next to Jacaa. Chessa hopped off next, slipped forward, and scored a belly-flop slide into Mica's feet. At first she made no movements, but then a furry paw shot into the air with a triumphant 'thumbs up.'

"Come on, sis. It's a snap," Mica said, signaling with his arm for her to follow.

As Madison prepared to step off of the lift, it abruptly dropped several feet, causing her to fall over the side.

"Maddy!" Onyx screamed as she raced toward the shaft where her friend disappeared. Like a baseball player sliding home, she slid on her knees all the way to the edge where she stopped herself just before going over. She reached down with one hand to see if she could reach

Madison, but the elevator had dropped down too far. "It's too far, I can't reach!"

The elevator floor was several feet below Onyx's level, and Madison dangled under it, holding tightly onto the edge of its floor.

"You *have* to help her!" Mica said to Jacin, who was still on the elevator.

"Okay," Jacin said. "How's this?"

Like a mean kid in the chair stopped on top of a Ferris wheel with a passenger who disliked heights, Jacin began to jump around. This started the elevator swaying to and fro.

"I—*hate*—you!" Madison struggled to speak, straining to keep any kind of a grip on her slippery handhold.

Hanging several stories up in the elevator shaft, Madison looked down to consider the distance between her and the bottom. It was then that she noticed the photo of her grandfather and the queen she'd carried in her pants pocket was about to fall out. Not about to let this hard won piece of evidence get away, she released one hand so she could secure the photo that meant so much to her.

"What are you doing?" Onyx asked.

"I can't lose my…." Madison's voice trailed off as she finally secured the picture back inside her pocket.

"You must join us up here, Miss Terrence." A hooded figure stepped forward into the dim light. "You see, you have something of mine." Mourgla raised his hand toward the elevator and it began to rise slowly until Madison was hanging above them. But, she continued to rise higher and higher still.

"Enough!" Mourgla bellowed. Lucian and Scratchley could be heard down below, blaming each other for pulling on the rope too hard. They lowered her back down where she could safely swing over to join everyone else.

Jacin hopped down, beaming with personal satisfaction and great pride for having delivered his captives to Mourgla. While he was expecting much praise and many rewards for what he considered a job well done, what Jacin got was little more than a nod of acknowledgment.

Mourgla slowly and deliberately moved around the children like a mountain lion stalking small game. He looked them over briefly and then stopped to face Madison.

"There's something about you." Mourgla hissed as he leaned toward her. "I detect a growing energy, a new energy coming from you. Interesting indeed."

Mourgla reached out and ripped Madison's necklace with its gem from her throat. As he held it up to the light, he told the story of fifty years ago.

"I was only hours away from Krybos being mine, when Queen Marcelene enlisted the help of a surface world dweller named Rocky Terrence, your grandfather, to save her precious world. Somehow, he managed to do just that."

"That's right, mister," Mica said. "My Grandpa kicked your butt!"

Madison reached around Mica's shoulder and pulled him closer to her, hoping to get him to shut up.

The hooded figure stared down at Mica, who was

causing his glasses to dance on his nose from the awful faces he was making. Unconcerned with the tiny menace, Mourgla continued, "But what really caused me the most pain, was what Rocky did next. While he was in the mountain of Zaltana, he created a series of safeguards to prevent me and others—whose purposes were not entirely pure—from ever getting in there again. Then, when he emerged, he split the Ashclaw crystal into three pieces and scattered them between your world and mine." Mourgla placed the gem securely in the pocket of his robe and patted it softly with his hand. "It's taken me fifty years to get back to this point, and I will not be thwarted again."

"Now that you have all of the pieces, you don't need us," Madison pleaded. "Let us go."

"As you say, I do have all three crystals," Mourgla said. He slid his vein-painted hand from his pocket of Ashclaw pieces and rested it over his chest where his heart would be, if he had one. "What I don't have is pure intentions. That's where you come in."

Mourgla went on to explain that Digby would be placed in a cage suspended over a pit full of fanged lizards, particularly vile creatures called farks. Mourgla warned them that, in a short amount of time, the lizards would have Digby out of the cage and torn to shreds. That is, *unless* the kids entered the Crystal Chamber and reset the tower for him. If that were the case, Mourgla said he would free Digby as soon as they had completed their task.

Back at Elea, Rocky and Digby sat in silence as the horror played out on the sensing spike. Rocky was in a state of disbelief that his grandchildren, Onyx and Chessa had become victims of his old rival, Mourgla.

Mica looked over at his sister and knitted his eyebrows together, then shook his head very slowly back and forth. He didn't want to draw Mourgla's attention, but he wondered if Madison realized what had just been said. Chessa had not spoken, even when they captured her, so Mourgla would not have known that he had the wrong gopher. Mourgla thought he had Digby. Madison and Onyx both appeared to be aware of Mourgla's mistake, but they kept quiet. Jacin, as usual, had no clue.

Reluctantly, the kids agreed to take the three pieces of the Ashclaw Crystal into the Crystal Chamber, but only with the secret hope that they would be able to come up with a plan to save Chessa before time ran out, for her and for Krybos. The dank air in Mourgla's lair hung thick with despair as Mourgla took Chessa away to await her fate.

Jacaa led the children to the kitchen where Lucian and Scratchley were already packing snacks for the journey.

After a quick glance around the trashed room, Jacaa looked at the horned cats and said, "Well, that certainly was quick work." He added, "Why go to all this trouble to get a head thumping, when I can offer you each a very thorough one for free?" Snickering, he turned to leave. "I'll be back," he added as he disappeared through the door.

Lost in thought, the kids began preparing for their upcoming trek across Krybos to the purple mountain of Zaltana. Mica struggled to get an extra apple into his overly-tight castle guard pants. He had several glowing light sticks already packed in his pockets, which he'd found in the castle guard's dressing room, so he didn't have much space to work with. He stuffed the fruit in just as Jacaa returned.

"It is time," Jacaa said. "Our journey begins."

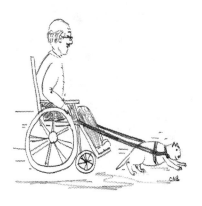

17
To Demelza

"There's no time to waste," Digby said. "Mourgla's got the kids and there's no telling what he might do to Chessa, since the fool thinks he has me." He turned and bounded through the gardens toward the main gate of the Step Castle, glancing back to see if Rocky was wheeling up behind him.

"Calm down, Digby," Rocky said. "We need to take a few minutes to decide what plan of action we're going to take."

Digby placed a paw to his cheek and tapped a few times while he stared blankly into the Script Stream that gurgled past him on its way into a tunnel that ran beneath the castle. "I've got it. How about I go over to that stinky, dark and cheaply decorated castle and make Mourgla regret the sorry day he was born—unless, of course, he was hatched."

"Well, whatever we do, we need to do it soon." Rocky said. "Let's go talk to Marcelene."

Rocky wheeled his way back into the castle where he and Digby informed Marcelene about what had happened in the garden.

"I feel responsible because I didn't take her necklace and secure it in the castle," Marcelene said, standing by the arm of Rocky's chair. "I hoped I'd transferred enough energy to her to keep her safe from Mourgla. But, she became frightened and pulled away, I guess, too soon."

"I should've never allowed her to possess the crystal in the first place so, really, it's my fault," Rocky said.

"I've waited so long to meet those children, and now, I fear, I may never see them again!" Marcelene tried to choke back the tears. "What will we do, Rocky?"

She didn't see how Rocky could possibly go up against Mourgla and his horned cats, when he could barely rise up out of his wheelchair unaided. And yet, it seemed he was their only hope since the castle guard never ventured beyond the gates of Elea, and would be no match for Mourgla out in Krybos.

"We'll be heading out shortly for a spectacular rescue mission, that's what we'll do." Digby had scurried to sit on Rocky's shoulder, and here he stood on his hind legs, throwing punches at an imaginary villain.

"We'll be fine, won't we Digs?" Rocky asked, adding a wink of confidence.

"Why soy-tan-lee," Digby replied, imitating a favorite television character.

The castle guard hooked Digby up with a harness that attached to the front of Rocky's wheelchair. After parading proudly past Marcelene and a gathering crowd of castle dwellers, Digby turned and headed out of the castle, with Rocky in tow.

They made their way past the main gates and across the countryside until they reached the Forest of Demelza that hid Mourgla's fortress. It was still light outside as they entered the forest, but that made no difference under the thick canopy of leaves. The Krybosian light that permeated everywhere else never, ever, entered the forest of Demelza.

Traveling through the dark forest, Digby strained against the harness even though Rocky tried to help by pushing sticks and limbs out of the way. He used his hands to help his wheels roll over rocks and any other obstacles he was able to see. The journey seemed an impossible task, but that didn't deter either of them. They pressed on through the dense brush until the forest opened up at Mourgla's fortress.

After carefully crossing a clearing, then approaching the structure with caution, Digby eased open the massive front door and poked his head in. After a quick survey, he and Rocky rolled quietly into the main hall, ever mindful that Mourgla and his horned cats could be around any corner. Slowly, they worked their way through the main floor of the castle, but found no one. After a careful search of every room on the first floor, Digby rolled Rocky into the open elevator to ride up to the next floor to continue their search.

One floor at a time, they climbed up through the fortress until they reached the area they had viewed on the sensing spike. It was the floor that had the rows of cells with bars instead of doors.

"This is where the kids were when Mourgla swiped Madison's necklace," Rocky said. Struggling, he bumped across the gap between the elevator and the floor, and looked around for any clue as to where they might have gone.

"Do you think they've already left for Zaltana?" Digby asked.

"Yep. It looks like we're too late," Rocky said. Disappointment covered his face. "This chair of mine slowed us down too much." The tone of his voice revealed a strong frustration with his disability.

Rocky willed himself to stand, struggling up from his chair. He leaned briefly on the wall beside the elevator before he had to return to the wheelchair he'd depended on for so long.

"We'll find 'em, Rocky," Digby said. He tried to put some confidence back in the one place where he thought it had always lived, in Rocky's courage and determination.

The two of them got back on the elevator and rode down to the floors below the main level, continuing their search.

"Cree – py!" Digby said, as he craned his neck around a corner to look down a long hall. His nervousness had begun to show, although he was usually a master of hiding it. Mourgla's lair had a way of making even the strong-minded and courageous somehow feel very weak and unsure.

"You ain't just a kiddin'," Rocky added. "This place would make Darth Vader cry for his mother."

They moved cautiously from room to room, not finding anyone. They were, indeed, too late. Mourgla and the children were well into their journey to Mount Zaltana and the Crystal Chamber.

But where was Chessa?

18
Into the Heart of Krybos

"Hurry along," Mourgla demanded.

Mourgla walked his captives out of the dark forest of Demelza and across the barren landscape of the wide plain separating Demelza and Zaltana. His long purple robe collected a layer of white dust along its bottom edge as it brushed the ground. Nightfall loomed heavily, and it became increasingly difficult to see.

Mourgla led the way. Immediately behind him were Madison, Mica, and then Onyx, relentlessly prodded along by Jacin. Jacaa stayed in the back. He'd become accustomed to being last and usually preferred it, since it kept him out of Mourgla's reach. Lucian and Scratchley, along with several other horned cats, lumbered along playing and batting at each other as they crowded around Jacin's feet. He tried to ignore them. Together, the group steadily moved across the vast stone desert on their way to the purple mountain of Zaltana.

Grandpa would know what to do if he were here, Mica thought. *Grandpa always knows what to do when there's trouble.*

Mica looked at Jacin and made a weird face, the kind he usually reserved for his sister. Madison walked slowly, obviously struggling to figure a way to save Chessa and still get out of the mess they had gotten into. She focused on their dilemma with such intent that she never noticed the pyramid-shaped rocks beneath her feet. However, Jacin noticed them.

"Cool." Jacin put a handful in his pocket. "I'll bet you don't have any of these in your freak show attic."

"You're quite correct, and shortly you'll know exactly why there aren't any of *those* in the attic." Onyx lifted an eyebrow and grinned, but she really had no idea what the rocks were.

"Why are you always such a jerk, Jacin?" Madison asked. With her hands deep in her pants pockets, and one grasping her grandfather's photo, she watched her feet as she walked. "No one in my family has ever done anything to you, and yet, you get in my face at every opportunity. You're always saying something bad about my grandfather, and you don't even know him. It's clear you have a problem, Jacin, and it's *not* me. It's *not* my family."

Jacin didn't answer. He just kept walking, every few steps tossing away pyramid-shaped stones as he dug them out of his pockets. He knew Madison was right.

The Terrence family had always been the target of

ridicule in Cavern City. Jacin's grandfather had worked with Rocky Terrence back when the quarry was still in operation, but for some reason, he hated Rocky. Stories were passed down to Jacin's father about Rocky and how kooky he was, and the evil things he had gotten into that forced him to close the quarry.

Jacin's father was a mean man who chose to believe and spread lies, rather than look for truth about anything. He passed that hatred on to Jacin, and he encouraged distrust of the Terrences. Since Jacin wanted his father's approval so desperately, he dared not go against him. That's why he took advantage of every opportunity to taunt Madison and her grandfather. Each attack on the Terrence family was really an attempt, by Jacin, to win his father's approval.

The daytime light had completely given way to strange darkness across Krybos. The soft glow from the night sky resembled moonlight and created a white shimmer across the stone desert. Shadows were well defined by the eerie Krybosian night sky, and Lucian and Scratchley took turns pouncing on each other's shadow. Just as Scratchley was about to land on Lucian's wiry shadow, the sky went dark, and the shadow vanished. No one could see anything in the complete darkness that consumed the land.

Phfft! A quick, swooping noise sliced through the silence. When the soft glow of the night sky returned, it brought with it the shadows of only those who remained on the stone desert floor.

"What in the cornbread heck was that?" Mica asked, looking around for clues as to what had just happened.

"I don't know. What's the matter with those two?"

Onyx asked, casting her eyes over at the two horned cats.

Lucian and Scratchley were cowered down, holding on to each other. They looked at one another and swallowed hard, then turned their collective gaze onto the group that followed behind them. Just as they had feared, one of the cats was missing. Vanished! Lucian began to tremble, and he and Scratchley bolted to Mourgla's side. They knelt at his feet and tugged at his dust-covered robes, whimpering, whining, and pleading to be saved. They knew too well what had blackened the sky.

"I didn't see anything, but I smelled a horrible stink even worse than that rodent Digby," Jacin said.

Mourgla looked down at his bumbling cats with contempt. He turned to Jacaa, and was just as disappointed to find him hiding behind Madison.

"That was the Revens," Mourgla spoke as he held his arms to the sky. "It is the great winged fog that lives in the purple mountain, and comes out only at night. Its eyes glow orange, but its body has no shape that anyone has ever been able to see. It moves across the night sky, snatching up those who dare venture out into the darkness it presides over." Mourgla leaned toward Madison and swung an arm out, wrenching his wrist and clenching his hand in a wicked gesture of capture.

"Oh, we'll be fine for now," Jacaa said trying hard to comfort himself. "The Revens has a snack to keep it busy for a while, and it shouldn't return to the mountain until morning. By then our purpose here will be completed."

With a sudden twist, Mourgla shook Lucian and Scratchley loose from the length of his robe. The trek to the mountain resumed with the nervous travelers watching overhead for the glowing orange eyes of the Revens.

With each footstep, the purple mound in the distance grew larger until it was a steep, dark mountain that rose before them. As they drew closer, Mourgla led the group to a cave entrance tall and wide enough to be used for an airplane hangar. Onyx curled her nose up and cast an accusing glance at Mica. A horrible stench wafted out of the cave and as it did it spread to envelope everyone it reached.

"It was the Revens!" Mica demanded. "I didn't do nothin'."

"That's what I smelled when that cat got snatched a little bit ago," Jacin added. "It kinda reminds me of your Grandpa's freaky, stinky attic."

"Naturally, the cave is going to smell like the Revens if the Revens lives here," Madison said. She walked past Jacin and stood bravely in front of the cave opening. "What else would you expect?"

Madison knew she was staring into the face of whatever was to come. This cave was the start of a journey that she, her little brother, and her best friend would have to take. But, it was a journey that none of them could be sure where it would lead.

19
Tunnel to Doom

Mourgla moved slowly and deliberately toward an elevated ledge beside the cave entrance. There he turned and sat down to address the group. He leaned forward to rest his hands on his robed knees, then fully straightened his arms and locked his elbows.

"If you want to see that gopher alive again, here is what you are to do," Mourgla addressed the kids. "Onyx, you will be the keeper of the stones. Mica, you will be the keeper of the instructions. Do not lose them, as they are the only way you will know how to adjust the crystal tower. Madison, you will be the one who resets the tower. And Jacin, you stay with them in case they need some firm encouragement. Jacaa and I will be waiting here at the entrance should anyone decide to back out."

Madison and Mica exchanged an anxious glance, each hoping the other would take that first step into the blackness of the tunnel before them. Usually known for her fearlessness, Onyx worked her way to the back of the group, trying to avoid being volunteered as the one to go in first. Her reluctance was not so much about fear as it was defiance.

Trying to impress Mourgla with his bravery, Jacin stepped in first. With a flip of his arm he motioned for the kids to come after him. With slow and cautious steps, the four worked their way through the winding tunnel. Deeper and deeper into the mountain they went.

Onyx noticed that the floor of the tunnel was not typical for a cave. Instead of the usual thud of feet on a packed mud floor, this floor crunched with every footfall. She asked Mica for a glow stick. When she cracked it over her knee, the florescent green glow grew bright enough to light the tunnel several feet in front of and behind the group. She held the stick down to the floor.

"Galloping gopher goblets!" She screamed.

"What is it?" Mica lifted one foot to look underneath.

"Bones," Jacin said. "Mourgla said the floor of this cave is covered with the bones of the Revens' victims."

"Rather like owl pellets, I'd imagine," Madison said. She passed her foot through a crunchy pile near Mica's feet, spreading the material around. She added, "In owl pellets, the fur and bones get regurgitated after the owl's stomach digests the meat off of them. Judging by the size of these clumps, this would have to be from a very big …." Her voice trailed off.

"He told me that the bones of anyone who'd tried to enter the chamber, but never made it past the challenges are here too," Jacin said. He seemed to delight in telling Madison this.

"What challenges?" Mica pushed his glasses securely up on his nose.

Jacin explained. "It seems that when your Grandpa was here many years ago, he created a very difficult series of challenges that must be overcome to gain access to the Crystal Chamber. Actually, Jacaa says they're more like riddles. Answer them correctly and you enter the chamber."

"And if you answer them wrong?" Onyx crossed her arms.

"Just don't get them wrong," Jacin drew an index finger slowly across his neck. "It's what Mrs. Merrix would call ironic. Your grandfather's challenges were designed to protect the Crystal Chamber, but now they could cost him his precious grandchildren."

Madison fought back the tears. She was mad and scared, but determined that Jacin would see neither.

"I can't believe you actually pay attention in Mrs. Merrix's class," she scowled. "Well, you're still a first class jerk."

The kids moved steadily forward into the mountain. Onyx took the lead, holding up one of Mica's glow sticks to light the way. Madison followed with Mica close behind, holding tight to her long ponytail. Jacin walked behind to prevent anyone from leaving.

They followed the tunnel as it curved left, and then turned right, when suddenly they arrived at a dead end. They had reached a solid wall of shiny wet rock. A beam of unnatural light shone though a crack in the ceiling above, illuminating the tunnel's end with a strange glow. Mica searched the walls for a handle or a button to open the tunnel wall, but found none. He ran a cautious hand over the smooth rock.

"Schist," Madison said.

"And my sister just said what?" Mica's mouth dropped in surprise.

"I said *schist*," Madison snapped. She gritted her teeth and glared at her brother. "It's a type of metamorphic rock that I'm sure you know nothing about."

Onyx stepped forward. "This tunnel was carved from sedimentary rock, you can see it plainly if you look at the strata." She moved her hand lovingly across the tunnel wall, and then turned to the dead end. "But here, you see, is a wall of schist, a metamorphic rock. These two rocks types are not usually found together like this."

"I guess this means we're done, right?" Mica asked.

"No, not necessarily," Madison replied.

"That's right!" Onyx said. "Someone must have put this wall here at the end of the tunnel, so someone must be able to remove it, as well."

"What about these?" Mica held up the instructions he was given. He was relieved that they wouldn't have to go any further, but he knew Chessa's time was running out.

"Those are for the settings on the crystal tower," Onyx said. "They won't help us get *to* the tower."

"Give me that," Jacin demanded. He tore the light stick out of Onyx's hand and dared anyone to move. Then he headed out to tell Mourgla about the dead end they had run into. As Jacin stepped out of the cave,

Mourgla stepped in front of him with arms crossed and his shroud-covered head leaning in uncomfortably close to Jacin.

"Where do you think you're going?" Mourgla asked.

It was clear Mourgla was annoyed, but Jacin wasn't sure if it was because of him, or the horned cats climbing and playing above the entrance to the cave. Jacaa cowered off to the side wishing to join in the fun, but knowing better.

"I came to tell you that we ran into a dead end." Jacin was sure this news would enrage Mourgla so he prepared for the worst.

"I expected as much." Mourgla looked to the sky. The changing weather signified a human presence, a presence he'd felt some fifty years earlier. Usually, the presence of an immature human, a child, didn't bring about changes in the balance of Krybos. But the presence of an adult human did.

"Go. I don't need you anymore," Mourgla motioned Jacin to head back out into the stone desert, alone.

"But, what about the dead end?" Jacin asked, hoping Mourgla might still find some usefulness for him. Anything would be better than going out into the darkness of that desert alone with the Revens stalking from above.

"You are the reason for the dead end, Jacin," Mourgla said. "Like me, you are not pure of heart. Without you, those Terrence brats will be able to get past that dead end." He motioned for Jacin to leave, along with the annoying hoard of horned cats, and begin their trek back to Demelza. Only Lucian and Scratchley were allowed to remain with Mourgla at the entrance to the cave. Secretly, they would have preferred going back to Demelza with the others where they could goof off, eat, and sleep.

Meanwhile, inside the mountain, the kids pondered the wall at the end of tunnel. Onyx stepped between Mica and Madison and placed her arms around them both. Together they stood, bathed in the overhead light.

"Look, Madison," Mica whispered.

On the wall in front of them a message materialized: "I am numerous in shape and size, but singular in color. Brightly, I follow. Dimly, I'm lost. What am I?"

"Great galloping groundhogs!" Madison exclaimed. "It's one of Grandpa's challenges."

Turning to Mica and kneeling down to his level, Madison took his hand and told him not to be afraid. She told him that together they could beat these challenges. Madison looked up at Onyx, taking a deep breath in preparation for whatever result their answer might bring.

"Do you remember what Mourgla said about having pure intentions?" Onyx asked. "Only the pure of heart can enter the Crystal Chamber. The mountain didn't reveal this challenge until Jacin was gone. It knows. It knows that Jacin came here with bad intentions, and that we've come with good. We have to go on. We have to do this to save Chessa."

Mica took a deep breath and said, "Let's do this, ladies." He giggled at himself for sounding like a line from one of Grandpa's favorite movies.

With a determined face, Madison paced and mumbled. She crossed her arms in front of her, then raised one hand up and tapped her chin with her pointer finger.

Mica paced as well but, as usual, not in his sister's footsteps. When she stepped left, he stepped right. The two looked like revolving targets in a carnival shooting gallery. Onyx stood directly in front of the wall and stared deeply at it, as if she could see past it.

"How about grass?" Mica asked with a giggle. "It can be different shapes and sizes and one color—green."

Onyx said, "No. Sometimes it's brown, and it certainly can't follow you."

Continuing with her thoughts about the riddle, Madison stepped into the light to stand directly in front of the dead end wall.

"Of course," she whispered.

"Well?" Mica peered over his glasses at his sister. Clearly disappointed that she might have figured out the answer first, he was equally curious.

"The answer is right here in front of us." Madison pointed to the floor in front of where they stood.

"I give up, already! If you know the answer, spit it out," Onyx insisted. "It will either kill us, or let us in."

The crack in the ceiling allowed light from an unknown source to enter the tunnel. It lit up the dead end wall from behind the kids, casting their shadows on the floor between them and the barrier.

"The answer to the riddle is *shadow*," Madison announced.

The three studied their shadows on the floor. Then in a show of agreement, they turned to each other. Madison and Onyx reached out and each took one of Mica's hands into theirs. Together, they took a giant step forward onto their shadows. They listened and waited for the unknown to happen, but there were no earthquakes, no magic doors.

Mica pulled his hand away and turned to tell his sister what a stupid answer 'shadow' was when, suddenly, the riddle on the wall dissolved away. A new message appeared: Passage Granted.

The kids were past the first challenge. There could be no turning back now.

20
Surviving the Challenges

Mica replaced his hand securely in his sister's, just as the floor dropped away. The kids were whooshed down a ramp and dumped onto a rock table in the center of a small, square room. The room's four walls each had a stone slab door decorated with intricately chiseled creatures. The only way out of this room had to be through one of those doors, but which one?

Madison swallowed hard. She remembered Mourgla explaining how choosing the wrong door would mean untold horrors to those who opened it. Only the true door to the Crystal Chamber would avoid the network of tunnels that the Revens lived in.

"I've been stuck with antlers," Mica said, his face grimaced in pain. Carefully, he tucked his hands under his behind to shield it from further pain. Mica ran his hand across the surface of the table beneath him. As if reading Braille, his fingers saw carvings of animals and strange shapes arranged in and around a carved triangle of rabbits.

Madison said nothing, but hoped to silence her brother with an appropriate glare.

Twinkling and groaning, the old rock table suddenly activated and, in doing so, launched the kids onto the floor. They landed on their feet and backed away from the table being careful not to get too close to the strange doors.

"Ok, sis. You got us here, now what?" Mica asked. He was still irritated that he had not been first to figure out the answer to a riddle that now seemed so simple.

Madison stepped toward the table and traced her hand over its interesting shapes. When she reached the large carving at the center of the table, she froze.

"Great gophers," Madison spoke softly. "Would you believe me if I said I'd seen a teacher draw this very symbol on the chalkboard, on the last day of school?"

Inside the circle were three hares arranged in profile to form a triangle, back to back, and with their ears joining in the center to shape a hole.

The edges of the table were also covered with carvings of various symbols and animals. Each carving was made of a translucent precious mineral. The green carvings were made of jade, the red ones of ruby, and the purple ones were cut into amethyst. Every color imaginable was represented in the array of carvings. Light shone up through them to fill the room with a multi-colored light show. Mica laughed at his sister's color-speckled face, and held his hands out to watch the rainbow dance of color on his own skin.

"I know this symbol," Onyx said as she approached the table. "It's called the symbol of the three hares, or rabbits. It's found in religions around the world, dating back to antiquity. What's strange about it is that it has baffled scholars and archaeologists as to how the symbol could have ended up in very different religions, geographically separated from one another. Now it's here, too. I wonder if this might be where it originated."

"Too weird," Mica added.

Mica grabbed his sister's hand and pulled it slowly away from the table. Onyx busied herself with the design, while Mica's attention was quickly drawn to a flickering holographic image that rose up from the table and hovered above it. One of the hares suddenly sat on all fours, then delivered a message.

"When you see me, you see little else. When I'm gone, all is revealed. Beware the wrong answer." Then the translucent creature sat patiently and waited for an answer, be it right or wrong. The hare seemed to be hoping the answer wouldn't be wrong, as if too many times he had seen the wrong answers given. Too many times.

Mica scanned for clues. "The answer has to be somewhere among the carvings on this table. I'm sure of it." His fear had been replaced with the excitement of a fresh opportunity to figure out an answer before Madison did.

Onyx's eyes darted back and forth from cow to snail, moon to lightening bolt, testing each as a possible answer to the riddle. Then she slowly stepped forward, and with a confident hand, she touched the symbol of a star.

"When you see stars, it's dark outside—so, you see little else. And when the stars are gone, all is revealed because it is daylight!" Onyx said confidently.

The star's glow grew brighter, and then the stone slowly receded into the table, disappearing from sight. With that, the room began to rumble and shake. It sounded like a train passing by. Suddenly, the kids heard the sound of steel screeching over rock. They whirled around to see a shiny metal bar blocking one of the doors.

"One down," Madison said in her high-pitched voice.

"Two to go," Onyx sounded relieved.

Turning their attention back to the table, they noticed that the holographic image was gone and had returned to its place on the table. Then the second hare rose up and presented another riddle.

"When we meet you'll hate the stink, but when I'm dead you'll love the pink. What am I?" it asked. "Beware the wrong answer."

"Well, Digby stinks while living," Mica joked.

Madison didn't respond. She was back in concentration mode again. When he saw his sister already working out the next riddle, Mica's determination to figure out the answer was reignited.

Mica knew he could do this. He decided that he just needed to concentrate more, the way his sister did. She could block out everything around her—telephones, people or whatever—when she was thinking. Mica began to give serious thought to the riddle. He repeated it over

and over in his mind. He carefully considered every symbol, every shape, every carving. This was a really hard
riddle. Would each riddle became a little tougher than
the one before it? Even Madison was having a difficult
time. Or was she? She reached out and touched the pink
crystal carving of a pig.

"A pig? Are you crazy?" Mica gasped. His eyes darted
around the room looking for whatever doom might befall
them. "You're going to get us killed! Sure pigs stink in
life, but why love them when they die?"

"Think Saturday morning breakfast with Grandpa,"
Madison beamed. She loved the process of problem
solving.

"Bacon?" Mica supposed. He looked relieved that his
sister *might not* have gotten them killed after all.

Just as the star had done, the pig's light grew brighter
and then it dropped deep inside the table, leaving a void
where its crystal carving once decorated the table. The
room trembled and moaned with more ferocity than
before. Just as the kids grabbed the table to avoid being
knocked off their feet, a steel bar, like a sword being
wielded by a giant knight, shot out from one edge of the
door beside them. It scraped across the front of the door
and came to rest on its opposite side. The steely sound
pounded in their ears.

With the elimination of this door as an entrance to
the Crystal Chamber, there remained only two doors.
There was one in front of them, and one behind them. If
the riddle of the third hare could be correctly answered,
then the last wrong door would be eliminated, leaving
only the true door to the Crystal Chamber.

The third hare rose up to present the final riddle. It asked: "I am made of nothing and not welcome many places I appear. You can't feel me, but you can fill me. What am I?" As the hare sat back to await the reply it added, "Beware the wrong answer."

The children studied the table. Together they considered every carving, but none seemed to work as an answer to the riddle. Mica was no longer worried about coming up with the answer before his sister. He just wanted *someone* to get it. They were so close, and yet they could go no further.

"One of these carvings must be the answer," Onyx said.

"I know, but which one?" Madison replied, her gaze never leaving the table. "And beware the wrong answer," she said, repeated the hare's warning.

Onyx considered a carving of grass, carvings of each animal, circles and squares, triangles and strangely angled shapes she had never seen before. Mica showed his sister a carving of some clouds on the table in front of him. But when Madison pointed out that clouds are made up of water, and water is not weightless, he waved his hand in a demonstration meaning to never mind.

The answer to the riddle had to be something that you couldn't touch since it was made of nothing. All of the carvings on the table had the same problem. None of them could be considered made of nothing. The children slumped to the floor in defeat, and leaned their backs against the table. Mica rested his head on his sister's shoulder and Onyx rested her head on Madison's other shoulder. They talked of home and their parents, and the good times they'd had on university geology trips. They talked about school and wondered what teachers they might have gotten this fall. Onyx wished she and her friends could return to her homeland one more time to see its soaring green mountains and lush valleys so much like those of Krybos.

"Maddy, I've never told you this," Mica said. "And I probably shouldn't now, but I've always wished I could be as smart as you."

"You *are* smart, Mica," she replied. Madison paused to shift herself into a more comfortable position. "Actually, there's something *I've* never told *you*."

"Really?" Mica asked. He glanced over at Onyx, who watched and listened intently for whatever the revelation might be.

"I wish that I'd spent more time just being a kid and having fun all of the time, like you do," Madison told him.

"Yeah, me too," Onyx agreed.

"Poor Chessa," Madison said. "We've really let her down."

"Maybe we should just make a guess," Onyx suggested. She looked over at one door, then the other.

"We could choose one door together, and then we can open it manually," Mica added.

Since there were only two doors to pick from, one in front of them and one behind them, they had a fifty-fifty chance of choosing the correct door. Together they would decide. If they were right, they would continue on to the Crystal Chamber and complete their task. If they were wrong, then the open door would seal their doom.

They would die and their bones would be added to those in the cave's entrance tunnel.

But if they chose poorly, Chessa would die too, since there would be no one to save her. Onyx pointed out that if they continued to sit on the floor and do nothing, Chessa would still die—since it was only a matter of time before the farks got to her. That is, if they hadn't already.

"Okay. Let's do it." Madison stood up and dusted the back of her pants.

"I'm in," Mica said as he stood up.

"You know I'm always up for an adventure," Onyx said. She took her place between her friends.

Together, the trio carefully considered each door. Both were made of solid slate. They were the same size, same color, same everything. Madison couldn't believe that her fate, and the fate of her brother, her friend, Chessa, and all of Krybos, had come down to *eenie, meenie, miney, mo.* She never liked childish games, and now her life depended on one. The irony made her long for Mrs. Merrix's English class.

Mica looked at his sister, and when she nodded her head, he proceeded to recite the rhyme.

"Eenie," Mica pointed at the door in front of them. Reaching over his shoulder, he pointed at the door behind and called out, "meenie."

Then it was back to the door in front for *miney.* The rhyme finished with *mo* landing on the door behind them. That was the door they would open. It held either the Crystal Chamber or unspeakable horror. They had to try.

"I did the rhyme, now you open the door," Mica stepped aside.

Madison and Onyx walked reluctantly over to the chosen door. Onyx swiped her sweaty hand across the side of her pants, and reached out for its huge handle. Madison was unnerved to see her friend, who was known for her fearlessness, now so frightened. She placed her hands alongside Onyx's and together they slowly turned the handle until it gave out a faint squeak, like that of a mouse teasing a cat. The sound surprised and frightened them. They froze. Taking a deep breath, Onyx adjusted her grip on the door. She was just about to pull the handle all the way down, when Mica screamed out from over at the rock table.

"Wait!" he yelled.

Startled, the girls released the handle and it snapped to its original position. They whirled around to find Mica standing beside the table with an outstretched hand inviting them to share his wonderful discovery. The three of them gathered around the table where Mica began to recite the unanswered riddle.

"I am made of nothing and unwelcome many places I appear. You can't feel me, but you can fill me. What am I?" Mica beamed. He knew the answer and, gloriously, could tell that his sister did not. Sweet victory! "Don't you see it? The answer has been right in front of us the whole time."

"Would you mind telling us what it is?" Madison asked.

"I can do better than that," Mica said. "I can show you."

On tip-toed feet, he stretched over the table with his chest pressed up against its bumpy, rocky edge. Mica reached one arm out and thrust his hand down into the hole at the center where the hares' ears met. Feeling for a handle, he grabbed it and pulled with all of his strength. The table groaned with the sound of aged mechanical parts being made to move after years of not being used. With a familiar steely scraping and one final crunching thud, one of the remaining doors was suddenly blocked, and the other swung wide open.

"Oops. That was close." Onyx gulped as she stared at the steel bar closing the door she and Madison had almost opened.

"The answer is hole!" Mica proclaimed with pride. "I knew that some kind of machinery was operating the bars to block the incorrect doors. That meant the same machinery would block the last incorrect door and open the real door to the Crystal Chamber. And you know, with anything mechanical, there is always a way to operate it manually. I tried to figure out where there might be a lever or a button, and since the only thing in this room besides doors is this table, that's where I looked. It's such a cool table, covered with precious minerals and carvings with lots of colored light shining through. And then there was this plain old hole. Naturally, I wondered why 'a hole.' That's when it occurred to me that the hole had to be the hiding place for a lever that operates those doors. And, more importantly, the word 'hole' answers the riddle."

"I am—you are—I don't know what to say," Madison stumbled.

"I believe the word you are looking for is *smart!*" Mica said. "You're trying to tell me that I am smart, just like you!"

Madison agreed, and promised never to complain about him taking his toys apart to investigate what makes them work, ever again. She realized there was more than one kind of intelligence. Learning can come from sources other than books. The combination of all their talents had brought them to this moment. Side by side, the three of them stood at the open door and stared into the prismatic beauty of the most magnificent room that had ever existed.

Onyx and Madison stood aside and extended their arms, offering Mica the well deserved honor of being the first to enter the great Crystal Chamber.

21
Jacin Returns to Demelza

While relieved to be away from Mourgla and Jacaa, Jacin's situation had not improved. He was stuck with a group of eight horned cats that annoyed and tormented him throughout the entire journey back to Demelza.

"If I was Mourgla, I would get rid of all of you morons," Jacin scowled.

He walked briskly across the great stone desert, trying to distance himself from the irritating cats that taunted his every step. The eerie Krybosian night sky cast a glow on the faint tracks created on his first trek to Zaltana. Jacin tried to concentrate on the ground ahead of him because he didn't want to lose the trail back to Mourgla's castle. Also, he didn't want to lose the protective shadows cast by that eerie night sky because he knew the Revens still roamed overhead.

The cats persisted in their antics. They took turns

pouncing across and in front of Jacin, causing him to stumble periodically. One cat meandered near his feet like a house cat begging for a saucer of milk. It finally wound in and out around Jacin's legs until it sent him flying, face first, into the hard ground.

"That's it," Jacin growled. The expression on his face made it clear that he planned to deal with these cats once and for all.

Resting his bony chest on the sharp, pyramid-shaped rocks, he lifted his head and swept an arm across his face to wipe the dust from his mouth. As he pushed himself up from the ground, the outline of his body disappeared from beneath him as a familiar stink filled the air. Within seconds, Jacin was covered in a mountain of horned cats, shuffling and diving to find safety at the bottom of the pile.

Phfft! Jacin heard that awful sound he'd first heard while following Mourgla to Zaltana. It was the gut-wrenching sound of someone being snatched up by the claws of the Revens. Or maybe, Jacin thought, it had hands, or feet. No one really knew since there had never been a single clear sighting of the creature described only as a flying fog.

Silence blanketed the stone desert. Not a sound could be heard, not even the sound of breathing. The cats lay motionless, each hoping to avoid being noticed by the creature with the glowing orange eyes. As Jacin looked through the tangle of horns, legs, and tails, he could see shadows returning to the landscape. The Revens was gone. It had left as quickly as it came.

"You can get off of me now, you stupid cats," Jacin demanded.

One by one, the seven remaining cats stood up, but didn't venture too far from Jacin's side. It had become obvious to him these guys weren't anything to fear. They looked frightening enough, but they were really only simple and playful. Mourgla kept them around mainly because of their usefulness in scaring and intimidating others with their appearance, but he treated them poorly. The cats only stayed with Mourgla because their evil looks made them feared and misunderstood elsewhere in Krybos. People ran for cover whenever they saw a horned cat. Women scooped their children up and hid indoors. Birds flying overhead would steer a wide aerial path around any areas with those cats on the ground. Like, Jacin, the cats were eager to be accepted.

Jacin led the horned cats on their long trek back to Demelza. As he entered Mourgla's lair, the cats took off for their part of the castle and left Jacin standing in the main hall. By this time, Jacin had decided he'd had quite enough of Krybos, and Mourgla, and the Revens. He was going back home, and he was going to find a portal to get there.

He began searching every tunnel-like hallway and every room. Slowly, he worked his way through the intricate system of tall stone halls, but with no luck. After opening twenty-two doors, he came to the room where Chessa clung to the sides of her cage suspended just out of reach of the farks. They appeared to be trying to make some sort of tool to reach the cage and pull it down to their level. For a moment, Jacin considered helping

Chessa but, true to his character, he decided against it—
since he was mainly concerned with helping himself.

He closed the door, leaving Chessa behind.
Continuing on, he reached a large room with a staircase
that spiraled up and out of sight.

"There it is!" Jacin said. "That's the portal."

He lifted one leg and placed a foot on the first step
of the beautiful staircase. It groaned under his weight.
The sound caught him off guard and stopped him in his
tracks. Quickly, Jacin convinced himself that the sound
was normal for an old wooden staircase, so he continued
his climb. Then, several steps later, Jacin felt the staircase
begin to tremble under his feet. He paused again.

Just as he decided to go back down, the staircase roared
to life and collapsed its steps. As the stairs beneath him
smoothed out like a slide, Jacin found himself slipping
down and around and through a trap door that opened
suddenly at the base of the staircase. Jacin disappeared
through the opening and, once it was shed of him, the
staircase shuddered and reassembled as it was before.

Thud! Jacin landed on his backside in a musty, stinky
room filled with stringy rotten rope. In the darkness it
seemed that every inch of the floor was covered in a layer
of twisted, stinking, rotten tangle. He stood up trying
to balance on the unstable mess while smacking at the
filth on his clothing. Jacin saw that the brown muck only
broke apart and smeared, but it smelled worse than the
Revens and Digby, combined.

He looked around for some means of escape, but saw
no windows or doors. The only light that entered this
tomb came in through the roof many stories above. He

had landed at the bottom of a tall tower at the center of Mourgla's fortress.

Jacin thought he saw small square openings in the walls half way up the tower, but they were far too high to be reached by climbing. Panic stricken, Jacin moved clumsily across the mangled layer covering the floor. His hands worked the surface of the walls methodically, feeling for some means of escape. But there was nothing. Jacin was trapped!

He had hoped to be home before Mourgla returned to the fortress, but now he thought he might never get home. He couldn't get out, and no one knew where he was.

22
The Crystal Chamber

"Remember that geode you had in Grandpa's Attic? You know, when you were swallowed up in that sea of snakes?" Madison looked at Mica.

"Uh huh. So?" Mica wondered what that had to do with anything.

"If we had cracked it open, this is what it would've looked like on the inside." She held out her arms as if she was home leading a tour of the family's cavern. "This is amethyst."

"A whole lot of amethyst." Onyx added.

They stepped through the door and into the Crystal Chamber. It was a domed room with walls covered in purple crystal points. The crystals were all shades of purple and every possible size. Some were as small as peas. Others were as big as basketballs. Some were as big as cars. Mica ran his hand over the bumpy crystal wall.

"I wish I had my camera," Madison said. She knew her parents would never believe that she had actually been *inside* a geode. She could hardly believe it herself.

In the center of the room, stood a lighted cylindrical tower that reached from floor to ceiling. Slowly and steadily, it rotated in place while making a muffled, grinding sound. From top to bottom and all the way around, the tower was covered with long crystal shards protruding out from it. Pure white light escaped through the crystals just like fiber optics. Some crystals stuck way out, far enough to knock a person over if they were standing too near the tower when they came around. Others were pushed all the way in, with not even a nub sticking out to grab onto. All of the shards had strange symbols carved into the ends. It was this current, particular configuration of crystals that made the tower work, and kept the earth's magnetic field and Krybos in balance.

"I guess this is it," Onyx said.

She reached into her pocket and slid out the three crystal pieces Mourgla had given her to hold. As Onyx clutched them tightly in her hand, she could feel them growing warmer against her skin. Soon they begin to vibrate, but she thought at first it might be her hand trembling. It felt as though the crystals were trying to put themselves back together.

The three walked over to the rotating tower and found the spot where Mourgla had said the three Ashclaw Crystal shards would fit once they were joined. Onyx brought two of the pieces together and they melted instantly into one.

"Wicked!" Mica said, forever fascinated with how things work.

"Yeah. That's what I'm afraid of," Madison added, uncertain how science could possibly explain what she was witnessing.

When the final piece was added it blended quickly with the others. Then, like a flash, the restored chalcedony bloodstone jumped out of Onyx's hand and into its nesting place on the tower, as if it were drawn by some kind of invisible force. Now, the only step remaining was the systematic realignment of the crystals as listed in Mourgla's instructions. Mica pulled the paper from his pocket. He studied it, then looked up at Onyx and his sister.

"Since we know how to get here now, we can come back and fix everything after we save Chessa, right?" Mica asked.

Madison knelt in front of him and said, "Think about this realistically. Do you think Mourgla is going to let us walk away? He knows we'll come right back in here and change what he made us do. He's not going to allow that."

"Great galloping grape gopher guts!" Mica exclaimed. "We went through all of this and we're going to die anyway?"

Madison didn't answer, but Mica could tell she hadn't given up yet. He handed her the instructions, and she and Onyx began studying the symbols on the paper. The tower whirled in the background. Madison knew their best chance would be to do what Mourgla had sent them to do, and then get out alive. But she also knew they would have to find a way to come back and fix the tower again, before time ran out for Krybos.

Together, the kids began resetting the tower. Onyx held the instructions and described the symbol on the first crystal, and Mica searched for it. When he found the crystal with that symbol on it, Madison would either push it in or pull it out by the number of notches that Mourgla had written down.

"Scorpion." Onyx called out.

"Over here." Mica said.

"Yeah. That's it. How many clicks?" Madison asked.

"Three clicks—out." Onyx replied.

Madison grabbed the icy cool crystal and pulled until it clicked three times. As this tedious process continued, each adjustment caused the tower's light to dim and its rotation to slow. Appearing not to be aware of the eminent death of the tower, they worked steadily while they talked of home.

Nearing the end of their instructions, Onyx reported that there were only two more adjustments to go. She told Mica to find the crystal with a ram's head on it, and then told Madison to pull it out one notch. Click! With that adjustment, the tower's light went nearly out. It was very dark and difficult to see.

"Is this a grass hula skirt or a flame?" Onyx asked, as she struggled to see in the poor light.

Madison joined her friend trying to make out the drawing on the piece of paper that she could barely even see. Waiting patiently by the tower, Mica was in no hurry.

"I'm thinking—flame." Madison said.

"Okay. I'm good with that." Onyx said. "The final adjustment will be to the crystal with the symbol of flame on it. When you find it, it must be pulled out all the way, however many clicks that takes."

The search began with the children looking at every crystal on the tower. To identify some of the symbols in the dimly lit tower room, they had to trace over them with their fingertips.

"I think this is it," Mica called out from behind the tower.

The girls felt their way around to where Mica stood. Together they compared the symbol contained in Mourgla's instructions to the symbol on the crystal. It was a perfect match.

"All or nothing time," Mica said.

Madison reached up and wrapped her hand around the crystal, and then paused. Mica placed his hand on hers. Onyx placed her hand over theirs and together they pulled until it clicked four times.

"That's it?" Onyx wondered aloud, expecting something dramatic to indicate their success.

Madison shrugged her shoulders and looked around for some sign that they had done the reset correctly.

Suddenly, the tower groaned to a stop. Its dimmed light turned red and pulsed like a heartbeat, as the tower seemed to let out a death moan.

An incredible silence followed. The only sound came from three human hearts beating loud with fear, fear of what they had done and fear of what would come. Madison grabbed the paper, and balling it up in her fist, she threw it at the tower in a useless act of defiance.

The ground trembled as the tower resumed its rotation. However, now it turned in the opposite direction. Its eerie red light pulsated and hummed. Fresh fractures shot through the crystal walls causing amethyst points to be shed all around the floor. It sounded like a million huge, glass marbles being dropped on a sidewalk. Madison tried to shield Mica from the falling crystals while he shielded his ears from the deafening noise.

It had been done. The tower had been reset, and the interior world of Krybos was set to collapse with Madison, Mica, and Onyx trapped deep inside the Crystal Chamber.

23
Chessa's Rescue

Trapped at the bottom of the stone tower, Jacin sat on a stinking, mangled mess and leaned back against the cold rock wall. He'd been there long enough that his mind had begun to deceive him. Or, had it?

What kind of stupidity is this? Jacin asked himself. Feeling a sudden movement beneath him, he stood up and stomped around. That's when he noticed that the ropes beneath his feet squirmed whenever the Krybosian night sky shone brightly into the depths of the tower imprisoning him.

Tripping on a rope that entangled his right foot, Jacin fell face first into the stinking mess. After a moment of complete disgust, Jacin pushed himself up and onto his knees then sat back on his heels while tugging at his soiled shirt. He turned the bottom edge of his shirt inside out then rubbed the filth from his eyes with the cleanest part.

When he finished, Jacin opened his eyes to see another pair of green eyes set wide apart—each atop a thin stringy stem—staring back at him.

"Agh!" Jacin screamed. He jumped to his feet and stumbled backward to lean against the uncomfortable cold of the stone wall.

The twisted ropes smelled like a sewer as they began to roll and raise their heads to reveal themselves. These were not ropes at all! They were worms that devoured trash or anything else that might get in their way. They were there to eat anything that was not wanted. This was a frightening problem for Jacin, who considered himself particularly *not wanted*.

"Help!" Jacin yelled. "Somebody, anybody!" He yelled with every ounce of strength he could summon. He knew those cats were in the castle somewhere and he hoped, if they heard his screams, they'd come to see what was going on. It seemed those obnoxious creatures were his only hope.

The more noise Jacin made, the more active the worms became. Several nibbled on his shoes while others tried to wrap around his legs and pull him down. Sometimes, when they jerked, a brown sticky blob shot out of the top of their heads and stuck to whatever it hit.

"Gross—worm snot!" Jacin felt queasy.

Noises in the fortress, high above him, went unnoticed by the screaming boy. However, his own cries were noticed by others roaming the lair that night. Two curious figures peered down through the tower, watching Jacin.

"This'll be a great show!" a small figure said, with much delight. "It's like a dream come true."

"Now Digby, you know we have to help him," Rocky said. He tilted his head toward his furry friend, then raised an eyebrow in disapproval.

"Aw, I know. I know," Digby said in his Scottish-like accent. "I was just hoping for a spot of fun, that's all."

Rocky raised himself out of his chair and called down to Jacin who was now frantically pacing about in the sea of nastiness. "Up here," he called out.

Jacin stopped and listened. He couldn't tell where the voice came from, but he knew its familiar sound. Rocky called down again, directing the boy to look upward. As Jacin craned his neck to see the top of the tower, he saw an old man and a gopher leaning in through one of the small windows.

"Who stinks now, worm-boy?" Digby said, wrinkling his nose and rocking his neck from side to side. He couldn't resist this chance to jab at Jacin, since Jacin was the one who usually delivered the jabs.

"Come on—you *have* to get me out of here!" Jacin pleaded for help. "These things are trying to eat me alive."

"Oh, no worries there," Digby replied. "They'll kill you first."

Digby took on a sheepish look as he glanced over and saw Rocky's expression. "Oh, all right," Digby said.

Without uttering a word, Rocky made it obvious that this was not the time for hard feelings or payback.

Digby disappeared from the tower opening and scurried down a narrow passageway. He returned with a rope held in his teeth, its length snaking behind him. He tied the rope around his midsection, stopping briefly to contemplate his increasing girth. Sucking in his round furry belly, he pounced onto the ledge of the window and allowed Rocky to lower him down to Jacin, who grew more frantic with each passing moment.

When he reached the boy, Digby removed the rope and told Jacin to wrap it around his own waist. Then, satisfied with the fine knot he'd tied for Jacin's safety, the plump ball of fur scampered up the rope to join Rocky, who stood leaning through the open window. His wheel-chair was turned on its side next to a large structural column in the center of an empty room. The rope around Jacin's waist rose up out of the tower and passed through the window. It stretched out across the room where it wrapped around the column and came back to where Rocky had fastened it to a wheel spoke on his overturned chair.

"Are ya' ready, boy?" Rocky called down to Jacin.

"Yes." He replied. "Can you hurry it up? P-p-please?" The last words tripped over Jacin's lips, having never passed from his mouth before.

Rocky and Digby cranked the chair's wheel, winding up the rope which caught and coiled on several metal nubs protruding around the wheel's outer edge. If Mica could have seen this operation, he would have been greatly impressed by the ingenuity of it all. In a short amount of time, Jacin stood before Rocky and Digby, very grateful for their unselfish help. He thanked them both with a sincerity neither had ever witnessed in the boy.

"Thanks, again." Jacin said as he tugged and worked on the strong knot Digby had tied.

"You're welcome," Rocky replied.

"That's the best knot you'll ever come cross." Digby reached up and slipped a tiny claw through a loop in the knot, then pulled it free.

"Why are you guys at Demelza?" Jacin asked. He was busy scraping the stinking slime off his clothes.

"We're looking for Chessa and the kids," Rocky said.

"And while we're here, we have some unfinished business with ol' mump-head Mourgla." Digby added.

As they talked, the fortress began to tremble softly, like a building when a train passes close to it. Rocky knew it meant the magnetic reversal was complete, and the earth strained from the forces created by the sudden shift.

"What is going on in this crazy place?" Jacin asked.

"It would appear that my grandchildren and their friend have solved the riddles guarding the Crystal Chamber, and have succeeded in resetting the crystal tower," Rocky said, putting his fingertips to his forehead. "It doesn't surprise me, really. But it means that we have precious little time now. First, we must find Chessa."

"The other groundhog?" Jacin asked. "I want to help you rescue her."

His face shone for the first time with genuine honesty and pride, and he liked how it felt. Still, he felt swallowed up by the feelings of guilt he felt for all the horrible things he'd ever said about the Terrence family. He was ashamed of all he'd done and was determined to try and make up for it in some way, starting right at that moment.

Jacin told about his trip to the mountain of Zaltana, and the dead end in the cave, and how he ended up back at Mourgla's castle. He told them how sorry he was for all he had ever said about the Terrence family, and for everything he'd ever done to them. He said he was sorry for his father's behavior, as well. For the first time in his life, Jacin really wanted to help.

"I've seen where she is," Jacin said.

As he described the room where he'd seen Chessa captive in the cage over that pit of farks, Digby lowered his head and slowly shook it back and forth.

"Oh, great," Digby said sarcastically.

"What is it?" Jacin asked.

"The stink is never going to come out of my fur," Digby replied. With the information Jacin had provided, Digby knew the best way to save Chessa was by going through the worm pile at the bottom of the tower from where they had just pulled Jacin.

"You mean the worms?" Jacin asked.

"Unfortunately," Digby said.

"Who's gonna' notice the smell anyway?" Jacin said with a laugh. "Just kidding, just kidding!"

Digby leapt onto the window ledge and stared down into the tangled mess at the tower bottom. Nervously, he fidgeted with the fur on the side of his leg as he considered just how hard that stink would be to remove. Then, he dove out of the opening and sailed down through the tower. He hit the worm pile with a splat, and within a few seconds his wriggling body disappeared under the writhing mess.

"Does he know where he's going?" Jacin asked.

"Digby knows this castle as well as you know your own home," Rocky replied. "He tunnels and explores everywhere he goes."

"Figures."

"Okay, let's go," Rocky motioned to Jacin.

The pair stalked their way through Mourgla's castle, with Jacin leading Rocky to the place where he'd seen Chessa in the cage. They made turns at the end of each corridor with caution, trying to remain unnoticed. Jacin really didn't think the horned cats would be a problem for them, since they hadn't bothered to answer his screams earlier. When they finally arrived at the door to the room where Jacin said Chessa was being held, they stopped and looked at each other.

"Rocky, I want you to know I am really sorry for everything," Jacin said.

"I know you are." Rocky reached out and placed a hand on Jacin's shoulder. "Now, let's get Chessa out of there."

The latch on the massive iron door felt cold on Rocky's hand. The straining of the earth caused vibrations to rumble through the ground and up through the castle. Rocky could feel it through the stone floor beneath his feet and through the handle in his hand. It seemed to be growing in strength.

Cautiously, Rocky lifted the latch and pushed the door open, but only wide enough to peek inside. Rocky leaned his head in and scanned left, then right. Jacin eased his head inside, just below Rocky's.

In the center of the room, they saw Chessa still imprisoned inside an ugly metal cage. A heavy chain suspended the cage over a circular pit, swarming with twenty or so small hairless rat-like creatures. These menacing brown farks had been working to figure out a way to get to the frightened groundhog. But, success for the dagger-toothed farks meant death for Chessa.

The farks launched themselves toward the cage and darted about frantically, trying to get to her. Several of the smarter ones climbed on each other's shoulders with the fark balanced on top, poking a stick into the cage's lock. Not one to give up, Chessa busied herself by shifting her weight back and forth inside the cage causing it to swing across the pit. On one pass she toppled the stack of lock pickers, sending them crashing to the hard floor. A small argument ensued among the smarting farks, as to who would be at the top the next time.

"Good show!" announced a familiar voice. It was Digby who'd arrived in time to see Chessa knock the farks over.

When Digby appeared in the fark pit riding a huge trash worm, the farks dispersed in obvious desperation. They scattered in every possible direction. Their fright at the sight of a trash worm made two farks jump so high they were able to grab onto the bottom of Chessa's cage. Once they realized where they were, they pulled themselves up and began grabbing at Chessa through the cage.

"Digby!" Chessa screamed, as she kicked at the vile creatures.

"Hold on!" Digby replied. He rode that worm in a loop around the pit, and then squeezed it with his legs. Like a rocket, the worm shot out of the pit and snagged both farks in its mouth as it sailed by the cage. "Trash worms love farks!"

Digby stood up on the back of the worm, and then

jumped from the pit to the floor, landing beside Chessa's cage. The worm backed away then turned to disappear behind several frantic farks escaping through the opening at the bottom of the pit.

"Are you alright?" Digby asked.

He looked up at Chessa who clung to the side of the cage, her face pressed between the bars to get a good look at her hero.

"I am now," she replied.

Jacin entered the room. As he moved toward Chessa, she snarled and retreated to the back of the cage. Jacin stopped when he saw her reaction.

"He's here to help, Chess," Rocky said. "It's okay."

"And he just happens to have a key to your cage," added Digby.

"I do?" Jacin asked, obviously confused by the suggestion.

Rocky nodded then cast his gaze to the pocket of Jacin's pants. Rocky knew that pocket held the locater crystal taken from his attic collection. Jacin suddenly became aware that the crystal in his pocket was icy cold.

"That particular crystal has a number of uses, and one of them is to open standard locking mechanisms like the one on Chessa's cage," Rocky said. "How fortunate that *you* should have one."

"Oh." Jacin placed his hand on his pocket, embarrassed.

Jacin walked to Chessa's cage, reaching into his pocket for the crystal he'd carried ever since his trip to the Terrence family attic. Jacin was just tall enough to comfortably reach the lock on Chessa's cage. Experimenting, he drove one of the crystal points into the keyhole and moved it about until it was well seated in the opening. Once fitted into the keyhole, the crystal's swirling center brightened and spun wildly, causing the lock to spring open.

Turning to Rocky, Jacin handed him the crystal and apologized for taking it.

"You can keep it," Rocky said. "It's yours now. It's a part of this world you can carry with you always."

"You mean it?" Jacin said with surprise.

"I mean it," Rocky replied.

"I'm rather glad you brought it!" Chessa said.

She leapt out of the cage, landing in Jacin's arms. He caught her, then knelt beside Digby and carefully set Chessa down, giving her time to steady herself before he let go.

"Thanks for coming for me, Digs." Chessa leaned in and nuzzled Digby.

"You know I'll always come if you need me," Digby replied. "Always."

Turning to Rocky, Jacin asked, "Now what do we do?"

Madison, Mica and Onyx were still in trouble and Krybos still faced destruction. The magnetic reversal had to be corrected before time ran out.

"There are only three who can save us and this world, now," Rocky said. "I hope I can reach them in time."

With his eyes tightly closed and his brow tense with deep wrinkles, Rocky looked like a man suffering from a bad headache. But Rocky's face didn't reveal what his mind had initiated. Touching his fingertips to his temples and lowering his head in concentration, he called out across the land, to the only ones who could save them.

24
Resetting the Tower

Deep inside the Crystal Chamber, despair hung like a thick fog, suffocating all it touched. The kids worried about the processes they'd set into motion with their final adjustment to the tower. They feared what might come next.

As they huddled together shielding each other from the crashing debris, a terrible shudder tore through the chamber. Like an earthquake, it shook the mountain. A wide gash ripped across the floor beneath them, sliced around the tower, then raced up both walls and tore open the ceiling. It was as if a geode had been cracked open and divided in two pieces. The split ran the width of the room and isolated Madison on the side with the tower, and left Onyx with Mica on the smaller side.

The floor's growing crevice crumbled along its jagged edges. As the kids scrambled back to avoid falling in, a steamy, hot wind howled and swirled through the room in a confused pattern. Its strength pulled at Madison, then pushed.

On the other side, Onyx pressed herself into a semi-standing posture, struggling against the force of the air currents that filled her nose with the horrible stink of sulfur. She was curious to see what lay at the bottom of the newly opened crevice in the floor. As she neared the opening, broken crystals disturbed by her feet were sucked in by the wind and tumbled away into the dark oblivion.

"Definitely not good," Onyx announced.

"Ya think?" Mica asked. He strained to steady his small frame in the brutal wind as he tried to stand and follow Onyx.

"Mica!" Madison screamed at her brother to get him to stop. She could see that he was losing the battle with the wind and risked getting sucked away. "You need to reduce your profile."

"Huh?" Mica asked.

"She means *get down*—out of the air current." Onyx turned and motioned for Mica to crouch down.

Mica crouched down and crab-walked his way backward to a safer distance.

Madison suddenly grabbed her head with both hands and rocked back and forth, seemingly in agony. Mica knew the noise from the tower and the wind wasn't bad enough to cause this sort of reaction in his sister.

"What's up with you?" he yelled across to her.

"It's Grandpa." Her weak voice trembled with effort to be heard in the increasing noise.

"What's that supposed to mean? Is something wrong with Rocky?" Onyx asked.

"No. It's a message from Grandpa," Mica said with excitement.

"He's talking to me." Madison said. She rubbed her forehead as if massaging would make the message clearer. "The message is—Chessa is safe – she's on her way back to the Step Castle – and now only *we* can save Krybos. It's all up to us."

"Grandpa must be in Krybos!" Mica's eyes flew open wide. "He's come here to find us. He always knows when we need him and boy do we need him now!"

"It's up to *us*?" Onyx asked. "You mean the lives of every living creature and person in Krybos is in *our* hands?"

The unshakable Onyx appeared quite shaken by the seriousness of the situation.

"Well, yes – I guess," Madison said. She stood and turned to face the tower.

"Grandpa is telling us to put the crystals back exactly like they…." Madison's voice trailed off, then instantly rebounded as she blurted, "Galloping grape gophers!"

"What now?" Mica asked, glancing sideways at Onyx.

"I believe your sister has suddenly remembered what she did with the instruction sheet that we now need to exactly retrace our steps to reset the crystals," Onyx said.

"Gees, I balled up the paper and threw it," Madison said as she looked down at the gaping chasm before her. "I'll bet it was the first thing to get sucked in."

"Good one, sis!" Mica pushed his glasses up. He

leaned back onto a huge crystal he used for a back rest. As he crossed his arms over his chest he added, "In case you're wondering, we're dead."

"Who gives up in the middle of their biggest adventure?" Onyx asked. "Not me, I can tell you that right now." She worked to make a path through the clinking purple piles.

"Well, I suppose it *could* be under this mess." Madison watched across the divide as Onyx searched the floor. She looked around on her side of the chamber, squinting to see in the dim red glow of the tower. To make matters worse, her ponytail elastic had fallen out and the wind kept forcing her hair into her face making it even harder to see. Naturally, she tried to work out in her head if the wind could blow her hair *into* her face, why couldn't it blow it *out* of her face? This made no sense to Madison, and she really liked things to make sense.

The floor was nearly a foot deep with heavy, sharp amethyst crystals that had broken off of the walls. On her hands and knees, Madison crawled through heaps of broken crystals on her side of the widening canyon. She sifted through the purple stones. Onyx crawled and searched on her side of the divide. Mica joined in and tossed around the smaller broken crystals that he could handle, hoping the instruction paper was wedged under the rubble. They tried to encourage each other in the search for the missing paper, but too much debris covered the floor. It seemed hopeless.

"Any luck?" Mica called out.

Madison didn't reply, but continued her search.

"It's getting too loud in here," Onyx said to Mica. "She can't hear you over there."

Madison came around the tower which stood dangerously close to the edge of the crevice. She stopped there to rest in the pulsating light. She could make out Onyx's form on the other side, and it looked to Madison like she was cupping her hands around her mouth and shouting at Mica.

"Don't move!" Onyx screamed. Then, she held out a hand gesturing for Mica to freeze.

"Ok, *now* what?" he asked.

"We're saved, is what," Onyx said.

Hidden beneath a mound of pinkish-purple, broken crystals, was a larger crystal with the misshapen paper jutting out from underneath it. Luckily, the chunk was heavy enough to have anchored the paper in the terrible wind.

"When I say push, you push," Onyx said. She positioned Mica's hands on the crystal and her own as she prepared to free the instruction paper.

"Ready?" Onyx asked.

"Always," Mica said.

Onyx double-checked her death-grip on the paper. Then, with one hand by Mica's, and both feet anchored, she shouted, "Push!"

Across the chasm, Madison could see that Onyx had the paper in her hand so she waved a thumbs up sign.

With that, the kids were ready to reset the tower—except for one problem. Onyx, Mica, and the instructions were on one side of the deep opening, and Madison and the tower were on the other. They had to get to the other side.

"It's too windy to throw the paper," Onyx said. "We'll have to jump over to the tower."

"I knew that was coming," Mica scrunched his nose up and studied the ever-widening canyon that separated them from Madison and the tower. "You first—you're the adventurous one."

"Okay. But after I cross, you must follow."

"No problem," Mica swallowed hard.

Onyx removed one shoe, then crammed the paper deep inside her sock so that it was snug against the sole of her foot. When she replaced her shoe she gently patted it like a new puppy. "It's not getting out of there."

Making her way to the edge of the divide, she crouched briefly to judge the distance across. She also considered the drop. It was too dark to see the bottom and too loud to hear if material dropping into the depths ever reached the bottom. Somehow, Onyx still knew it was a long way down.

She got into a sprinter's starting position and rocked back and forth a few times. Then with an explosion of energy, she sprang across the span, hoping to land well past the crumbling edge.

"Woo-hoo!" Mica cheered when he saw that Onyx had safely made it. His excitement soon faded into terror when he realized it was his turn. He swallowed hard, again.

Madison and Onyx motioned for him to follow. By this time, the gap had opened wider and presented an even bigger challenge than Onyx had faced. This was not lost on Mica. He hunkered down near the edge and tried to summon the strength to make the leap.

It's just a hole, that's all. Mica told himself. *Probably only deep enough to stand up in.* Just then, a light stick tumbled from his pocket. *That certainly was convenient,* he thought. He picked up the stick, cracked it, then shook it into a bright glow. He released his grip and allowed the wind to pull it from his fingers and into the depths of the crevice. He watched for a full minute as it rode the currents and disappeared out of sight without ever reaching the bottom. Once again, he swallowed hard.

Mica steadied himself. Summoning all of his strength and courage, he made an Olympic-quality leap and soared out across the crevice. As he neared the other side, Mica realized he was losing momentum and tried frantically to flap his arms like a bird in flight. Madison and Onyx also realized his plight and threw themselves down at the weakening edge of the canyon and reached for him.

"No! Stay back!" Madison screamed to Onyx. "You must keep the instructions safe and stay with the tower. One of us must survive and reset the tower."

"She's right," a voice rose up from inside the crevice.

Onyx shuffled back from the edge.

Mica didn't quite make it across, but when Madison crashed onto her stomach and slid to the edge of the canyon, she'd managed to grab his hands as he reached for the rim. He dangled just out of Madison's sight, his small body swayed with each violent updraft and sucking downdraft that swept in and out of the opening. With each swing, he pulled Madison a little further across the floor of the cavern, and closer to going over the edge with him. Her arms ached from the scratches inflicted by the broken crystal shards littering the floor, and her clothes were torn and sliced.

Madison caught a glimpse of movement out of the corner of her left eye, so she turned her head to see what it was. To her horror, the photo of her grandfather and the queen had come out of her ripped clothes and was hopping along wildly on the air currents. It was the only proof she had that her family was not crazy, and now it was only seconds from disappearing, forever.

"Great gophers!" Madison yelled in her highest-pitched voice.

She tried to release one of Mica's hands and grab onto the photo but, when she did, a wind current grabbed him and nearly jerked him out of her other hand. She retook his hand as more of the crevice edge loosened and dropped away beneath her arms.

"What are you doing up there?" Mica shouted from below.

After a brief pause, Madison replied, "The right thing!" She watched as her cherished photo took to the wind and rode the current up through the massive crack in the ceiling. Then she renewed her grip on both of her brother's hands, and with the strength of an athlete, she pulled him up and over the edge. She fell back and he landed on her.

"Wow! Who knew you could be such a brute?" Mica said. He could see Onyx laughing over by the tower. Madison, however, was not amused.

"You can get off of me now!" Madison said.

Mica made his way over to the tower, while Madison

thought about what that photograph could have meant to her. It would have put to rest the rumors and speculation about her family. She could have presented proof of a wonderful new world that existed deep inside the earth—a world that her family had once saved. Now, she was right back where she started, with one notable exception. This world was about to end if she and Mica and Onyx didn't act quickly to save it.

Madison joined them beside the slow turning tower where Onyx had removed the instruction sheet from inside her sock. She held tightly to a corner section that protruded from the crumpled ball, while Madison and Mica began peeling back and smoothing the sheet. With the instructions once more in hand, they could now reset the tower. Together they worked backward through the steps, identifying and adjusting every crystal until each one had been returned to its original position.

The howling winds gradually died out leaving only a renewed sound coming from the tower. With the beauty of a crystalline wind chime, the tower sang out with a melody of beautiful tones as its dim red light was replaced with a pure white light beaming through the crystals, splendidly lighting the Crystal Chamber as before. Satisfied that the restored tower rotated as they had first found it, they breathed a collective sigh of relief.

"We did it!" Mica said.

"Now, we are supposed to destroy the Ashclaw Crystal, then get inside the tower," Onyx said, surprised that she'd received the message from Rocky in her mind. "I think, obviously, splitting it is not enough."

"*In* the tower? Maybe we're not getting the message

right. There's no getting in that thing. Maybe he is saying to get *on*," Mica studied the tower.

"No, he said *in*," Madison insisted, verifying the message she'd also received.

The confusion was suddenly settled when the tower mysteriously opened to reveal a hollow interior. Mica knew right away he was looking at an elevator. Taking action, he plucked the chalcedony bloodstone from its nesting place on the tower and laid it on the smooth side of a large piece of amethyst.

"Now, to bust it up," Mica said. He loved when things came apart. Quickly, Mica scanned the area for an even bigger piece of amethyst with which to crush the troublesome crystal.

"Are you sure we should do this?" Madison asked. "I mean, to completely destroy it?"

Her hesitation resulted from an emotional attachment to the section of Ashclaw Crystal she'd worn around her neck. It was almost a familiar friend.

"Oh yeah, I think we should do it," Onyx chimed in. Normally not one to fear much of anything, her recent experiences of being captured by Mourgla, surviving the riddles, and resetting the crystal tower were events she did not *ever* want to repeat.

"You're both right," Madison agreed. She reasoned that with the Ashclaw Crystal completely destroyed, Mourgla could never try to take over Krybos again, at least not that way.

The kids found a huge amethyst point, as large as a soccer ball, and together they wrestled with it until they held it high above the Ashclaw Crystal. The crystal now lay exposed on the flat plane of the huge amethyst. Madison cautioned Onyx and Mica to avoid the exploding shards of crystal by squeezing their eyes shut tight, right before the moment of impact. Then, together, they counted off— one, two, three—and they let go.

The amethyst point plummeted through the air and landed directly on top of the Ashclaw Crystal, pulverizing it. In its destruction, the energy it held emitted blinding streaks of light that lit up the entire Crystal Chamber. Everyone turned away to shield their faces.

All across Krybos, a beam of pure white light could be seen bursting up out of the mountain and streaking toward the sky. This band of light made a roaring sound as it shot out of the mountain top. Mourgla and Jacaa had been standing on each side of the entrance to the cave when they looked up to see what was happening.

"Why those meddling, double-crossing…," Mourgla mumbled.

He knew what the kids had done and, before he could dive into the shelter of the cave, he and Jacaa were caught in the "feeler" streaks that reached out from the main light source. Instantly, they were transformed into hideous gray stone statues, standing on each side of the entrance to the cave. Lucian, who had been sitting at Mourgla's feet at the moment of the energy burst, became fused to Mourgla as their transformation occurred. Scratchley and Jacaa were also fused into a single statue which stood on the opposite side of the cave entrance from Mourgla and Lucian.

The intense surge of light died back until it was

completely extinguished, leaving the Crystal Chamber illuminated only by the light of the restored tower.

"Groundhog City, that was sick!" Mica said with a satisfied smile.

"You know, the energy that came out of that crystal didn't vanish," Madison said. "It went somewhere."

"But where?" Onyx wondered.

Madison knelt and searched the dust of the pulverized crystal for any traces of her beloved gemstone. She raked her fingertips through the residue, but nothing recognizable remained. She scooped up a handful, examined it closely, and then slowly tipped its contents out to trickle back onto the dust pile.

"I don't know, but I hope it's for good, not for bad," Madison said.

Satisfied that the crystal was destroyed and Krybos was saved, the kids turned toward the tower's open door. Mica hopped inside and started poking around to see what wonderful mechanics made the tower work. After Madison and Onyx squeezed themselves in, the tower door closed, sealing them inside.

Madison placed a firm hand on Mica's shoulder and said, "Whatever you do, don't fart. I mean it, little brother!"

25
Back to Elea

Morning soon arrived on the heels of that sky-piercing burst of energy emitted during the death of the Ashclaw Crystal. The kids worked so diligently, they didn't realize that they'd spent an entire night in the Crystal Chamber, trying to save Chessa and Krybos. When the tower elevator jerked to a stop, the door opened to a lush field of purple flowers, high on top of Mount Zaltana. Madison and Onyx dove out and rolled on the ground, gasping in desperation, while Mica slinked out laughing hysterically, holding one hand on his stomach and slapping his knee with the other.

"Whew! That's better than anything I've ever done." Digby weighed in on the quality of the odor oozing from the small tower elevator.

"Digby?" Mica ran to his furry friend and lifted him into a tight hug. "You won't believe where we've been."

"Grandpa!" Madison exclaimed. She and Onyx ran and hugged Rocky and recounted their harrowing tale of adventure and danger. Then, Madison's voice trailed slowly off into silence. She drew back and studied her grandfather, from top to bottom. Onyx quickly realized that something miraculous had occurred.

"Grandpa, where's your wheelchair?" Madison looked down at her grandfather's legs holding him up just as they had before the stroke that had put him in the wheelchair. The purple flowers surrounding him were rapidly fading as color drained from the blooms. Madison folded her arms around herself as a shield against the gusting wind which was ripping petals from their flowers and launching them into the sky.

"How's this possible?" Onyx asked.

Grandpa led the children over to the edge of a rocky outcropping, and then motioned for them to sit with him. He told them about the healing powers that Krybos holds. Mica wanted to know if it was some kind of magic, but Grandpa quickly pointed out that just because something is different than what you are used to, it doesn't mean that it is necessarily magic. What seemed to be magic on the surface world was only normal in Krybos. He said he owed his healing to the intensity of the earth's magnetic field which created a powerful energy flow in Krybos.

"Here," Grandpa said, "the field is so strong it enables the human body to heal itself quite rapidly."

"Have you always known this?" Madison asked. "If you knew that coming back here would help you to walk again, why didn't you come back sooner? You can come back any time that you want to, right?" Madison struggled to understand.

"Yes, I can come back any time, " Grandpa said. "But when surface world people—grown-ups in particular—are in Krybos there is usually a cost, just as there is when Krybosians come to the surface world. It's a matter of balance. The people and creatures of Krybos meant more to me than whether or not I could walk." He lifted one of his legs and presented it for inspection.

"That's who your Grandpa Rocky is," Digby hopped onto Rocky's lap. "He's a man willing to make sacrifices for those he loves."

Sliding a hand smoothly over Digby's back, Rocky continued. "I chose to stay in the surface world and only visit my friends in Krybos by remote viewing. It was when I noticed your tracks in our cavern that I contacted Marcelene, and she told me that Mourgla had brought you here. I knew had no choice but to come back."

"Well, I'm sure glad you did!" Mica said.

Grandpa looked all around then gazed up at the Krybosian sky. He sighed and said, "Oh, I have missed this place. It's been fifty long years."

"But where's Mourgla?" Mica asked.

"And what happened to Jacin?" Onyx asked.

"Jacin has returned to Elea with Chessa," Digby said. "He helped us rescue her and they're waiting for us at the Step Castle."

"Jacin helped someone, you mean, other than himself?" Madison asked in disbelief. "Good grief!"

"It's true, Maddy." Grandpa said. "And Mourgla, he's

just over the hill a bit, where you put him into safe keeping with his pals. I'll tell you everything back at Elea."

"We got him with that flash of energy, didn't we?" Onyx asked, already knowing the answer. "I knew it!"

"Let's go." Grandpa said, motioning toward the stone desert. "It's getting dark early because of my presence here, and we don't want to be out at night in Krybos."

"You're not *even* kidding!" Mica looked to the sky.

Grandpa led the group down the mountain and across the barren stone desert, back to the Step Castle at Elea. They hopped, skipped and ran, testing Grandpa's restored abilities. As they approached the city wall, the gates of Elea creaked open to reveal Marcelene and Chessa, eager to welcome them back.

"You did it!" Chessa cheered. "You saved our world!"

"We did it, we did it, uh huh, we did it!" Mica sang with pride as he marched in step to his victory song.

Chessa led them over to waiting boats. Once everyone had taken their seat, they floated on the Script Stream, through the gardens and then along a tunnel system that ran beneath the castle. The smell of roasted meat seeped into the tunnel and filled Mica's nose.

"Somethin' sure is smellin' good!" Mica said.

"A magnificent feast has been prepared in the Temple of Doom Dining Hall, to celebrate Mourgla's defeat," Marcelene said. "The people of Elea are grateful and they invite you to join them. I am grateful as well and I invite you all to sit with me – at the main table."

As Marcelene winked at Grandpa Rocky, Madison

detected a connection between them that, she suspected, was not something new.

Grandpa agreed they would stay for the celebration, but insisted that afterward they must leave in order to preserve Krybos' delicate balance, and to prevent any further harm. The weather had already begun to alter, and soon it would have an adverse effect on plant and animal life.

The flat, raft-like boats followed the winding tunnel system until they were directly below the center of the castle. Water lapped the boats' sides and splashed the small docking area as, one by one, their riders hopped out to follow Grandpa. He appeared to be quite familiar with the castle. Together, he and Marcelene led the kids to the dining hall. As the small group entered, the sound of grateful cheers and applause rang in their ears. They made their way to the main table situated at the front of the hall, where Jacin was already seated.

"Hello, Jacin." Madison felt obligated to acknowledge his presence, but could barely manage to speak as she glared at him.

"Calm down, Maddy," Grandpa said. "I said I would tell you everything." Grandpa motioned Mica and Onyx to take their seats, and then he called for Madison to come sit by Jacin's side.

"Great," she mumbled to herself. "I plummet down a stairpath portal into a new world, risked life and limb trekking across Krybos to the Step Castle, got captured, was led across a plain where the Revens haunts the night sky, survived life and death challenges and the near total destruction of Krybos, and my reward is to sit with Jacin Means at dinner?"

But, Madison couldn't believe it when she heard of Jacin's role in Chessa's rescue. She had never imagined him capable of any degree of kindness.

"I've come to realize that, while my father is a harsh man who prefers to lash out at everyone as a form of communication, I'm really not that kind of person." Jacin shifted in his chair, obviously nervous about how Madison was taking his revelation. "It took me coming here, to this world, to figure that out."

Madison fidgeted with her place setting, adjusting the positions of silverware that had already been set perfectly, and making every effort not to make eye contact with Jacin. She feared that if she did, she'd see he was only lying, and she wanted so much to believe he had changed.

"Hello? Madison?" Mica called out.

Onyx placed her hand firmly on Mica's shoulder and steadily increased the squeeze until she had his attention. He peered up over his glasses, then pinched his forefinger and thumb together, drawing them across his lips to show he'd shut up.

"What I'm saying is—I mean, I want to apologize to you, and your whole family, for all I've ever done or said," Jacin said. "I'm really, really sorry."

Madison slowly moved her attentions up from the table, and looked at Jacin. She stared into his eyes for what seemed, to him, to be an eternity. Then, without uttering a word, she rose from her seat and turned to face everyone.

"Jacin, on behalf of myself and my family, I accept your apology." She rotated back toward him as she finished her sentence.

With that, Jacin sprang to his feet, offering his hand in friendship, which Madison readily accepted, as the crowd cheered. Marcelene and Rocky sat together, beaming with pride.

"This place really is magic," Madison said.

"No, Maddy," Jacin replied. "Not magic, just different."

26
Return to the Stairpath

After the celebration, everyone gathered in the center of the city where Marcelene opened the stairpath portal, just like the one that had brought the children to Krybos. Dressed in her royal finest, she sat high in a pink marble throne, piled with gold-trimmed, jewel-toned cushions. Mica thought she had to be the most beautiful queen ever.

"Madison, Mica, Onyx, and Jacin," Marcelene spoke. "Please come." She motioned for them to stand before her.

Mica looked a little intimidated, as though he had been called to the principal's office. However, he took reassurance in his sister's fast response to the queen's call. The children took each other's hands, Madison holding Mica's and Jacin's hands, and Onyx holding Mica's other hand. Together, they approached the throne, then stood there quietly.

Marcelene stood and walked to the edge of the throne's wide circular platform, then said, "Krybos owes you all a huge debt. Without your brave actions our world and our people would surely have died."

The crowd of onlookers cheered, with Digby doing an impressive version of a "polo cheer" from the movie *Pretty Woman*. Marcelene encouraged the crowd to celebrate freely and enjoy the moment. Once they had quieted down, she continued her speech.

"I want each of you to leave with something to remember us by. Jacin, step forward, please."

Jacin took a step toward the queen and waited anxiously. Marcelene stood at the edge of the platform, and handing Jacin a book, she said, "This book contains many secrets. It contains many answers. It contains many questions. It will decide which you require each time you open it. Anytime you need help in the future, just open the book. Carry it with you, always."

Marcelene patted Jacin on the shoulder then motioned for him to step back and allow Onyx to step forward to claim her reward.

As Onyx took her position in front of the queen, Marcelene motioned for a small bag tied with string to be brought forward. She held the open bag out for Onyx to reach inside.

"In this bag, you will find what looks like an ordinary ring," Marcelene said. "This ring, however, allows you to contact me from wherever you may be. You've been in the Crystal Chamber and now Mourgla knows who you are. It is unlikely, but should he *ever* be able to break free of his stone prison, you could be in great danger. Wear this ring, always."

Marcelene patted Onyx on the shoulder and motioned for her to step back. Then, she turned away and returned to her throne. Madison looked over at Mica who had turned to look at her. They both wore equally sad and confused faces. How could *they* not get a reward? The queen had said *each* of them.

Just then, Grandpa Rocky walked across in front of the kids and took his place up on the platform, standing beside his queen. Together, they motioned for Madison and Mica to step forward.

Grandpa spoke, addressing Mica first. "I guess now you must realize that I'm not that great a storyteller, since my stories were all true. I doubt if I could've ever made up tales as exciting as the adventures I've had here."

"It's okay, Grandpa," Mica said. "I like your stories—even better, now that I know this place is real. And cooler than that, now I've got some stories of my very own to tell!"

Turning to Madison, Grandpa said, "I know you've struggled with the rumors that have long been associated with our family. To me, they were just harmless fun stories of adventure in a place no one knew about. But now I realize, to you, they weren't just fun stories. They created a fountain of unanswered questions and were a source of confusion."

"If I'd only known it was all real, then maybe…," Madison spoke, then her voice trailed off. She realized it didn't matter now. She knew the truth behind the stories and she was okay with it.

"I intended to tell you guys everything when you got older but, I guess, time caught up with me," Grandpa said. "Anyway, since the stories were real, there is some truth to what the people of Cavern City were saying. But, they were dead wrong about us being involved with anything evil. With the exception of Mourgla, Krybos is good, and thanks to your help, he is no longer a problem. As for your struggle to understand...."

"Please, allow me," Marcelene interrupted, placing a soft hand on his. She stood and walked gracefully, queenly, to the edge of the platform. There, she stepped off the edge and sat back, using the platform as a seat. She invited Madison and Mica to come sit on either side of her.

"Maddy, I know you've been struggling with your identity lately and searching for answers," Marcelene said. "I know this because I *know* everything. Just like you *know* everything. That's because we are the same, you and me."

"The same?" Madison asked.

"I, too, remember everything I see or read," the queen said. "Like you, I learn instantly that which takes others months or years to learn. And like you, my thirst for knowledge is unquenchable. You see, that incredible mind of yours was inherited."

Madison cut a confused gaze over at her grandfather and waited for confirmation. He smiled back at her, nodding his head in agreement.

"Madison and Mica, I am your grandmother." As

she spoke those words, not a sound could be heard other than Digby sniffling at the happy moment. Just like his pal Rocky, he, too, was the protector of those kids, and he loved them dearly.

"Whoa! Dad is your kid?" Mica asked, somewhat in disbelief.

"Yes," the queen said. "And that is why, just like those of us here in Elea, you are noticeably shorter than most people. That trait skipped your father, but he passed it on to you. The intellect trait was passed to your sister."

"Snap!" Mica said. "I thought I was really different because I am short. But it turns out that I'm the *same*, the same as the people of the Elea and the Step Castle."

Marcelene continued, "Your grandfather remained as long as he could, but ultimately, he couldn't stay here in the interior world. And I couldn't go with him to the surface. So, when Jim was born, I sent him to live in the surface world with his father, your grandfather. I felt like Jim would be safe from Mourgla there, while we'd hoped his presence in the surface world wouldn't create too much of a disturbance. He's only half Krybosian."

"Does my father know you're his mother?" Madison asked.

"Yes, sweetie," Marcelene replied, taking Madison's hand in hers. "Jim knows."

"Jim has always known who his true mother is," Grandpa added. "He's even been here a time a two as a child, but for the most part, he only makes contact from the attic or the cavern."

"I suppose the birthday gifts he waits desperately

for each year, they're from you?" Madison looked to Marcelene.

"Yes, he sure does love crystals and odd artifacts," she said. "And I never miss a birthday."

Turning to Grandpa, Madison asked, "But what about Nana Terrence?"

"I met your grandmother, Ruby, when Jim was about one-year-old," Grandpa Rocky said. "I was lonely and we fell in love then were married a short time later. Ruby couldn't have children, but she was a good mom and raised Jim like he was her own. Then, she got sick and died when he was in high school. I never remarried."

"It's all rather unbelievable!" Madison said, contemplating the startling revelations. "I planned to get some answers this summer, but galloping groundhogs! But, you know what? I'm good with it!"

"Yeah! We're royalty and didn't even know it." Mica reached across his grandmother and high-fived his sister.

Reaching into a pocket, Marcelene retrieved two large clear orbs, each about the size of a baseball. She handed one to Madison and one to Mica. As the children took hold of them, the orbs began to glow green then hum in their hands.

"Call me, sometime?" the queen asked.

"Ah, snap!" Mica said. "A Krybos cell phone!"

"Good grief, Grandpa." Madison said. "Are we really taking this dweeb back to the surface world with us?"

"So, how 'bout a hug for Grandma?" Marcelene stretched out her arms and both children folded into them.

Just then, the Step Castle shuddered as a loud crack

echoed up through the staircase portal, prompting a sharp gasp from the crowd.

"Okay guys, it's time," Grandpa said, holding an arm out and hurriedly motioning with his hand for the children to join him. Nodding his head toward the straining staircase portal, he added, "I've overstayed my welcome."

"Do we have to go?" Mica asked.

"Sometimes choices must be made based on what's best for all, not just self. It's always the way, and will always be the way – we can't stay. Even when it's the only thing in the world that seems important, we can't stay," Grandpa said, stepping onto the first stair tread. Turning, he motioned for the kids to proceed up the steps ahead of him.

"I love you two dearly and will always be watching out for you," Marcelene told her grandchildren. "You must make your way back to the surface world now. Always remember me?"

"We will!" Madison and Mica said in unison. They hugged their grandmother one last time and walked over to the staircase.

Onyx waved goodbye to everyone then began to lead the way up to the surface. She was followed by Jacin who was waving to his new friends, then Madison and Mica followed. Mica stopped to look back at Digby, who was sitting with Chessa.

Mica knew that his best friend intended to stay behind, in his own world, so he ran back down the steps and scooped Digby up into his arms. The gopher couldn't speak, but it wasn't because he'd lost his language skills.

This time is was because Mica was squeezing him so hard that he could barely breathe.

Mica set Digby down and told him, "I love you Amon Ossian Zollicoffer. I'll miss you."

With a final hug, Mica left his friend and started back up the staircase, trying not to look back. Grandpa waved a final goodbye and began following the kids up the winding staircase, to the surface world.

As Chessa watched Digby's face, she could see that he wanted to go back to the surface world, to the *real* adventure. She knew he could never be truly happy, unless he was tunnel digging and watching movies with Rocky. Chessa leaned over and kissed him on the cheek. Digby looked deep into her eyes, and could see that she finally understood him. This time, she wanted him to go, and to be happy.

As Digby started to pull away, Chessa reached out to touch his paw and said, "Just remember, a staircase that descends, rises from somewhere. Don't forget *from where.*"

"I won't," Digby whispered.

The ecstatic gopher darted over to the staircase and shouted up to Mica, "Before I lose my ability to speak and must be content with making gopher noises, there is something I'd like to say."

"What's that?" Mica's voice echoed down from high on the staircase.

"The name is Digby. My friend Rocky gave me that name."

With that, the people of Krybos watched that familiar furry tail curve its way up the staircase, and out of sight.

Contact Information:

SRR Colvin can be contacted through her web site:
www.srrcolvin.com

She can also be reached by e-mail at: srrc@srrcolvin.com

Author's Notes

Virginia has over 4,000 known caves, but not all of them are open to the public, and for good reason. Cave exploration is a dangerous activity for people, and can result in tragedy. And sometimes, it's the caves that need protection. Cave exploration is an activity that is best left to the professionals.

There are, however, many commercial caves that are open to the public and provide guided tours. Eight fabulous examples are in western Virginia, lining the I-81 corridor. They are:

- Crystal Caverns
- Dixie Caverns
- Endless Caverns
- Grand Caverns
- Luray Caverns
- Natural Bridge Caverns
- Shenandoah Caverns
- Skyline Caverns

A brief list of geology terms and definitions, as well as links to relevant web sites, can be found at www.srrcolvin.com.